"What happened on the dance floor shouldn't have happened."

"I know," Cayden interjected. "That situation was way too public and, because of that, ended way too soon."

Avery was stunned speechless.

"Neither of us had making out in mind when we stepped on the dance floor. It just happened."

"I know. That type of behavior is totally not me," said Avery. "I felt guilty about what happened. Then I was confronted in the bathroom. That was my exit cue."

"Her name is Teagan. I'm sorry about that."

"Either way, I apologize for getting caught up in the moment."

"If I apologized, I'd be lying. I very much enjoyed what happened that night."

"It can't happen again. Intimate interactions with Point Country Club clients are not permitted."

"What about when those persons are no longer clients?"

* * *

Inconvenient Attraction by Zuri Day is part of The Eddington Heirs series.

Dear Reader,

From the time Cayden Barker meets Jake Eddington at ten years old, he becomes that brother from another mother who feels like family. He practically lives at Jake's house. With trouble at home and since Jake's family have unofficially adopted him, Cayden permanently moves in at fifteen. So close is their bond that his story begins this new series featuring the shenanigans of the risk-taking, money-making Eddington heirs!

For this series, I've left Nevada and the West Coast, where both the Drakes and Breedloves resided, and moved to the Midwest. Point du Sable is the überexclusive fictitious suburb just outside Chicago where Cayden first runs into Avery. Or is the other way around? Either way, sparks fly in both directions. Have you ever met someone who rubbed you in every wrong way but for all of the right reasons? That's what happens with these two, although it takes a while for them to realize it. Which is where your journey with this couple begins. Welcome to Point du Sable! Welcome to The Eddington Heirs.

Please enjoy and always remember to...have a zuri (beautiful) day!

Zuri Day

ZURI DAY

INCONVENIENT ATTRACTION

HARLEQUIN
DESIRE

HARLEQUIN®
DESIRE™

Recycling programs for this product may not exist in your area.

ISBN-13: 978-1-335-73532-4

Inconvenient Attraction

Copyright © 2021 by Zuri Day

This edition published by arrangement with Harlequin Books S.A.

For questions and comments about the quality of this book, please contact us at CustomerService@Harlequin.com.

Harlequin Enterprises ULC
22 Adelaide St. West, 40th Floor
Toronto, Ontario M5H 4E3, Canada
www.Harlequin.com

Printed in U.S.A.

Zuri Day is the award-winning, nationally bestselling author of a slew of novels translated into almost a dozen languages. When not writing, which is almost never, or traveling internationally, these days not so much, she can be found in the weeds, literally, engaged in her latest passion—gardening. Living in Southern California, this happens year-round. From there it's farm to table (okay, patio to table—it's an urban garden) via her creative culinary take on a variety of vegan dishes. She loves live performances (including her own), binges on popular YouTube shows and is diligently at work to make her Ragdoll cat, Namaste, the IG star he deserves to be. Say meow to him, stay in touch with her and check out her exhaustive stash of OMG reads at zuriday.com.

Books by Zuri Day

Harlequin Desire

The Eddington Heirs

Inconvenient Attraction

Sin City Vows

Ready for the Rancher
Sin City Seduction
The Last Little Secret

Visit her Author Profile page at Harlequin.com,
or zuriday.com, for more titles.

You can also find Zuri Day on Facebook,
along with other Harlequin Desire authors,
at Facebook.com/harlequindesireauthors!

Sometimes love comes when we least expect it.
We have no control or a way to direct it.
Impossible to dictate our heart's reaction
When we get caught up in an inconvenient attraction.

One

Technology wizard and financial phenom Cayden Barker's already bad day just got worse. He never saw it coming. "It" being the car that had just sideswiped his nearly new super-sporty Porsche and sent it on a 360-spin into the intersection and a forceful awkward meeting with a light pole. Cayden was tossed, turned and jostled, but too immediately angry to feel any pain. Without a thought to his health or safety he jumped out of his car to survey the damage. The innovative aluminum all along the car's right side—a material used to decrease the weight and increase the speed—now resembled the crinkled foil his mother used to cover Sunday leftovers. He felt light-headed and placed his hand on the car's hood to prevent a fall.

"I'm so sorry! Are you okay?"

Cayden whirled around. Bad move since his head kept spinning after his body stopped. He steadied himself once again before waving his arm toward the damaged frame. A woman's face with wide pretty brown eyes etched with concern swam into view.

"Do I look okay?" He jabbed a finger at the passenger side's crushed hood, door and fender. "Does this look okay?"

"Police and ambulance are on their way. Perhaps you should sit down."

"Perhaps you should learn how to look where you're going!"

"Please calm down, Cayden. You're bleeding."

It didn't at all register that she'd used his name. His hand went to his head in a reflexive move. He looked and saw blood, along with another shade of red. Anger.

"What in the hell is wrong with you!"

"The sun's angle. I couldn't see the light—"

"If you can't see, you shouldn't be driving!"

"I tried to stop."

Cayden walked around his customized baby, its unique paint now streaked by dented gray metal. It had taken the dealership three months to create the exact shade of blue he'd requested, navy with a subtle gold sheen, and another week to repaint the exterior. Everything from the mirrors to the stainless-steel steering wheel to the kid-leather seat coverings were customized, had been special-ordered from all over the globe. He'd driven the car less than a month. Now here it sat—shattered, crushed—much like his ego after the earlier executive meeting. The light at the end of that dark and unexpected tunnel was the lunch he was having with a longtime mentor. The lunch for which he was now late. His anger, already at ten, soared off the charts. He felt like a thundercloud and was ready to storm all over the hapless motorist who'd ruined an already very bad day.

Except something stopped him.

Her eyes.

The look in them—fearful, apologetic. The tears that shimmered, giving those deep brown orbs a coppery tone. Only now he imagined how six feet and three inches worth of seriously pissed-off must have looked to a woman almost a foot shorter in height. He took a deep breath to calm himself and stepped out of her personal space.

"I'm truly sorry," she said again, looking from his crumpled dream of an auto that had set him back six figures to her boatlike clunker that other than a busted light and bent fender showed not a scratch. "Whatever my insurance doesn't cover…"

Cayden waved off the rest of the sentence, glad he'd taken his best friend Jake Eddington's advice and purchased the company's top-notch auto insurance package that covered the car from tip to tail no matter what happened or who was at fault. The movement brought his watch into view and reminded him that a businessman with no time to waste was waiting for him at a nearby restaurant. From the wording on the text messages that led to the meeting, it was one he dared not miss. Just as sirens were heard in the distance, he reached into his suitcoat pocket and pulled out a card.

"I've got to go," he said, holding it out to her. "Do you have a card with your contact information?"

"Yes, but…" She looked around. "Aren't you going to wait for the ambulance and police? That cut should be tended to and we need to make a report."

"You know what happened. As long as you tell them the truth, there shouldn't be any problems."

The woman hesitated only a moment before walking to her car. She reached inside for her purse, sifting through the contents as she returned to where he was standing. Instead of the business card he was expecting, she pulled out a pen and began writing on a fast-food receipt.

"What's that you're driving? It barely shows signs of the accident while my car needs to be towed."

"My grandmother's Buick, at least twenty years old."

Buick or battering ram? Cayden was sure the body was made from steel and could have subbed for a WWII tanker.

"I would have traded it except it belonged to her and Granddad."

Or because it could survive the apocalypse.

"I've just started a new job so no business cards yet. But here's my name, number and—" she reached inside her wallet and pulled out a card "—my insurance information."

Cayden took the slip of paper. "Avery Gray."

"Yes, that's…me."

He looked up again, took in her face. There was something remotely familiar about her, but considering the tons of people he met at social and professional events, and given that he'd spent much of his life in the upscale atmosphere of Point du Sable, a conclave of less than ten thousand citizens just north of Chicago, he could have seen her or someone closely resembling her anytime, anywhere. Plus, Cayden never forgot a pretty face and even with its distraught expression, Avery's features were pleasant, soothing even. It had distracted him from being livid, stopped him from dishing out a verbal lashing and had him standing in the street next to his wreck when he should have called an Uber or hailed a taxi five minutes ago.

Flashing lights brought Cayden out of inaction. He watched EMTs exit an ambulance and saw the tow truck operator engage his hazard lights before jumping from the cab.

"My insurance company will handle this. Slow down and watch where you're going. Okay?"

"Definitely."

The female EMT walked directly to him, her eyes glued to his forehead. "That's a nasty gash you've got there. Are there other injuries?"

"I'm fine," Cayden said, backing away from her and looking at the tow guy. "Make sure she's okay."

Cayden continued to his car without waiting for a response. He talked briefly to the tow truck driver, while calling for a ride. When the Uber driver pulled up a short time later, the police still hadn't arrived to take the report. Cayden couldn't worry about that. With the unexpected pushback he'd just battled at the office and whatever news his mentor was going to share when they met, a busted forehead and smashed-up car, even one as expensive and fly as his custom Porsche, was the least of his worries.

Once inside the car and on the way to the restaurant, Cayden texted details of the accident to his agent and requested a rental. Then he looked in the mirror. The driver who'd hit him, Avery, had been right. So had the EMT. The cut was bad, deeper than he'd thought and nastier looking than it felt. He used sanitizer and Kleenex the driver provided to clean the blood from his face, and covered that on his shirtsleeve with the soft charcoal wool of his tailored suit jacket, but he still felt far from the

GQ persona he usually presented. A short time later, the greeting from his mentor confirmed what he felt.

"You look like you were in a dogfight…and the dog won."

"Pretty much, Mr. Masters," Cayden replied, a slight smile causing a few hearts to skitter as he shook the older man's hand. "Except it was a car fight. My Porsche versus a car made before the turn of the century."

Bob Masters, a gentleman of distinction whose toned, upright carriage, smooth skin and thick wavy hair belied his seventy years, chuckled.

"Chevy?"

"Buick."

Bob shook his head. "Then condolences for your ride are probably in order." He returned to his seat and directed Cayden to the other side of the booth. "I doubt it can be brought back from the dead."

"Unfortunately, you might be right." Cayden winced as he sat, the pain he'd felt on the car ride over shooting up again.

"Are you okay?"

"I will be."

"You sure you don't want to go to Emergency, get that gash and other possible injuries checked out? When it comes to automobile accidents, you don't feel the pain until the shock wears off. That cut above your eye looks pretty nasty."

"You said this meeting was important."

"It is, son, but not more important than your health. As you get older you'll come to realize that nothing is more important than that."

"I'll stop by Mom's on the way home. Have her look me over."

"How is Tami?"

"Still saving the world."

"She still at IMCOC?"

The Illinois Medical Center of Chicago is where Cayden's mom, Tami, had worked for twenty years, and where she and Bob had met.

"She's at PDS Medical now. Getting a job there is the only reason she finally agreed to move."

"She's living here now?"

Cayden nodded. "A two-bed, two-bath condo in Harold Washington Heights."

Bob's brow raised. "A Kincaid property?"

"I tried to talk her out of it but she loved the layout and the location being so close to her work." The briefest of frowns marred Cayden's good looks before he shrugged. "Before moving in, she burned sage."

The server arrived. Mild laughter at Cayden's remark was followed by casual chitchat as drinks were delivered and orders were placed. Cayden endured the curious stares and a few polite interruptions as elite members of the community paid due respect to one of the town pillars. He was anxious to get on with the meeting and learn why he sat calmly hiding a now-splitting headache and increasingly sore ribs, nursing a ginger ale, when he probably should have been in an emergency room with someone attending to him. The salad finally arrived and with it a slight shift in Bob's posture and change of expression that signaled the talk was about to get serious.

"You're familiar with the Society."

Cayden leaned forward. "Of course."

Everybody who was anybody knew about the ultraexclusive business fraternity, the Society of Ma'at, whose roster of members read like a who's who of the world.

"At a recent meeting, your name came up."

As he thought of the possibilities behind being mentioned, Cayden's brow creased.

"Relax, my boy. It's good news."

Cayden released the breath that only now he became aware of holding.

"New membership is open."

"That only happens every five years."

Bob nodded. "Normally that's true. Unfortunately, we are no longer living in normal times. In the past year we've lost several key members. The organization has had to adjust, along with the rest of the world, and voted unanimously at our annual meeting to hold a special vote for new members. I felt the time was right to nominate you for the club."

Cayden's back hit the booth seat with a thud. Not a good move for the rib almost surely broken. He was too shocked, too moved, to feel a thing.

"Wow, Mr. Masters, this is an incredible honor. I don't know what else to say."

"It is actions, not words, that qualifies you for the brotherhood. Philanthropy, community service, fundraising for worthy causes. Along with professional success, and exemplary social standing, those are the types of activities that we use to elevate our community."

Cayden nodded but said nothing.

"On or around every major holiday, Society members across the country plan and host major fundraisers for charity. I'd like you to put one together for the Fourth of July."

"Me, sir?"

Bob's grin was slow and compassionate. "You can handle it."

"I've attended functions like that but wouldn't know where to begin…"

"That's what mentors like me are for. I'll guide you along the way, but I want it to be your work. Golf tournaments are always big hits, especially if we can host it at the Point."

Cayden relaxed. Golf he could do, and as for Point du Sable's exclusive country club, the Eddingtons practically owned it. He was sure that with their help he could secure those eighteen holes for his event.

"I think I can put something together."

"Not just something," Bob said, his fingers steepled on the table before him. "Because of its connection to the Society, it must be the biggest, baddest summer event in all of the Midwest."

"I'll get on it right away."

"That's the professional side of things. Now, regarding your personal life, the Society doesn't like scandal. Anything that mars the name of a member mars SOMA."

"I understand."

"Make sure that you do. From now on, every area of your life will have to be stellar, flawless, one hundred percent above any fray."

"I'll go above and beyond anything asked of me, sir. You have my word."

"I believe that. You'll get a letter in the mail soon, and then a phone call. After that your ninety-day probation will begin, followed by the vote taken at our national conference. On top of raising millions for charity, the event on the Fourth will be your unofficial coming-out party."

Cayden's steak arrived, seasoned and cooked to perfection. He didn't taste any of it. Later, when he stopped by his mom's house, Tami confirmed that, if not broken, his rib was severely bruised. She wrapped him up, cleaned his cut and suggested it might need a stitch or two. On the way home he played the voice mail of a call that he'd missed.

"Cayden, it's Avery. I know you said your agent would handle things but I still feel badly about what happened and just wanted to check on you. I stayed until your car was towed and the police arrived. You should get a copy of the report in the mail. Hopefully, you made your meeting and got that cut looked at. No need to call back. The insurance company said they'd be in touch. Take care of yourself and don't worry, I'll be the most attentive driver in town from here on out."

Cayden found himself smiling as he listened to her talk. A call from the woman who'd ruined his ride should have irked him, but instead he felt better. The strangest thing. By the time he pulled into his driveway, he'd chalked the good vibrations up to Bob's surprising news, the chance to become a member of the world's most elite business club. Deep down his feelings told him it was the woman who'd stayed on his mind since the accident happened. But that didn't make sense. How could someone who'd caused something bad make him feel good?

Two

"I can't believe he didn't recognize me."

Two hours after arriving at PDS Medical, and one hour into her sister's chemo treatment, Cayden was still very much on Avery's mind.

"You haven't seen each other since high school. It's probably a good thing. Considering everything that happened with Brittany…"

"What does that have to do with me?"

Lisa gave her younger sister a look. "We were all friends back then."

"And he was a jerk."

"All of what she said happened got retracted, don't you remember?"

Avery shook her head. "I thought he got off because of his Eddington connection."

"You might be right."

"It's horrible what he tried to do to her."

Lisa rested her head against the pillow, her smile weary. "Look, I'm not trying to defend him. Brittany was my friend, too, remember? I'm how you guys met. Something about that whole situation always seemed off. Is he still as fine as he was ten years ago?"

Avery thought about how her body had reacted when Cayden got out of the car, much as it had back in the day just about every time she saw him. How his body radiated power as he'd strode angrily toward her and his eyes, dark with fury, seemed to sear through her soul. Even in her distress, all of that had registered. Remembering it caused a certain set of muscles to clinch even now.

"He looks even better," she admitted, before remembering she'd taken a hiatus from men.

Lisa cleared her throat, her voice firmer when she spoke. "I remember when he and Jake used to come by the restaurant. They'd get the attention of every woman in the room, no matter the age, race, weight or height."

"Except you."

Lisa looked at Avery with one eye. "I wasn't immune. But he was too young for me."

"Brittany didn't feel that way."

"Brittany likes every man with a pulse. Cayden was thoughtful, mature for his age. He was always such a gentleman, a good tipper even then when he had to be, what, eighteen years old? That's why I found Brittany's story hard to believe. After seeing the retraction, learning she'd left town without so much as a text message and reaching out several times to her with no response, it didn't matter. We were done being friends."

"She didn't respond to me, either. I couldn't believe how she cut off everyone, especially you since you guys were so close. Even went ghost on social media. Obviously, she wanted to put the past behind her. Left, got married. Snagged a wealthy one from what I hear. Old Boston money."

"Yeah, Frank told me she made the paper's society page. Good for her."

"He's a member of SOMA."

Lisa signaled her whoop-de-do disinterest by twirling a finger in the air.

Avery smiled and stood. Lisa had never been into status, though being a member of the Society of Ma'at fraternity was as high a status as a man could get. She walked over to where her sister lay on the bed. Lisa wasn't a big woman to begin with so the weight she'd lost during the chemotherapy treatments grew more noticeable each day. She reached over and smoothed Lisa's thinning curls away from her pallid face.

"You're probably tired." Lisa nodded as her eyes fluttered closed. "I should let you rest through this and come back when you're done."

Lisa shook her head. "It's okay. Frank texted me earlier. He can pick me up."

"He didn't have to work overtime?"

"He rechecked the schedule. It's tomorrow night."

"Okay, then." Avery placed a hand on her neck and rolled it around.

"You need to get that checked out."

"My neck? It's just a little stiff. I'll be okay." She leaned over and kissed Lisa's cheek. "Hang in there, okay. I love you."

"Love you more."

As Avery reached her car and headed out of the parking lot, the red neon emergency sign beckoned in the distance. She twisted her neck and shoulders and thought about taking her sister's advice. Then she thought about work and her boss, Maggie, who was going on maternity leave in three short weeks and would be out for twelve and decided against it. What if a doctor determined she should be admitted? She'd just gotten hired. There was no way Avery could take time off from the job. She remembered how Cayden had been so committed to making his appointment that he refused medical help. Given that comparison her neck didn't feel so bad. She stopped by a drugstore, purchased some ointment, took a hot shower and called it a night. The next morning when her alarm went off, she could barely move.

Well, isn't this just great?

She patted her nightstand for the cell phone placed there, found it and called her boss.

"Perfect timing," was Maggie's greeting, way too chipper for this time of day and the neck that caused pain upon movement. "I was just getting ready to call you."

"Sounds like you've been up for a while."

"Yeah, the baby woke me up a couple hours ago. She's made the inconvenient decision to try to come early. Glad you weren't hurt in that accident yesterday because I'm at the office and need you here, pronto."

"Ow!"

"I know, you're not a morning person."

"No, it's my neck. It was a little sore yesterday but today I can barely move it."

Silence on the other end of the line.

"Don't worry, Maggie. I'll be there. I just need to get this checked out, possibly get a brace and maybe a prescription for the pain. Shouldn't take more than a few hours."

"I'm sorry, Avery, but I don't have that long. The doctor has ordered me off work. I'm only here long enough to gather a few things so that I can work from home. I'll be on semi bed rest until the baby's delivered. If you can't make it, maybe I should call—"

"No. Don't worry about it. I'm on my way."

Avery grit her teeth as she rolled out of bed and headed to the shower. It had taken her more than a year and several interviews to get a position at the Point Country Club, where it was possible to see and be seen by some of the most prominent business professionals, athletes and celebrities in the world. Those who were lucky enough to get employed there rarely left. Avery had no intention of letting someone replace her, even temporarily. It was the first time she'd felt good about herself in a long time. As much as the club needed a great event planner, Avery needed the boost that came with the club's prestige.

Just over an hour later Avery eased out of her trusty Buick, slipped through the club's employee entrance and tried to look as though she were walking normally while moving nothing but her legs. Now that going to the doctor wasn't an option, at least not today, it seemed her body decided to betray her. In addition to the stiff neck, she had a splitting headache and she'd be darned if while showering hadn't felt a pain in her back. But she reached the office and had so much information crammed into her brain over the next hour that words could have spilled out of her ears. She and Maggie were just getting ready to go over the appointment calendar when a contraction ripped through her boss's abdomen. She plopped into a nearby chair.

Avery rushed over. "Oh, my gosh, are you all right?"

"I—" *pant, breathe* "—think that—" *grimace* "—I need to go."

"Don't worry about the calendar. I'll handle it." Avery reached for her cell phone. "Who should I call to come get you?"

"I can…drive," Maggie managed between clenched teeth.

Avery knew that would never do. Maggie was in no condition to be behind her desk, let alone behind the wheel of something weighing more than a ton. She tapped the intercom.

"Charlotte, we need you…now!"

The next several minutes were a blur. Securing a wheelchair. Planning an exit that didn't include the front of the club. Even in an emergency like this, decorum was everything. Avery's stiff neck and aching body were forgotten. By the time Maggie had been secured in Charlotte's car and Avery headed back inside, she almost felt normal. Stopping to use the restroom on the way to the office, she recalled Charlotte mentioning a one o'clock appointment that had just been set up.

Did she mention a name?

Avery looked at her watch. Her eyes widened. At 12:56, it didn't matter who was coming, just that she was there to greet them and show them the type of hospitality for which the Point was known. She hurried out of the stall, washed her hands, fluffed up her waning curls and adjusted the spandex-style undergarment taming her folds into an hourglass figure and possibly causing the headache and pain in her back. Too late, she wished she'd thought to grab her purse to add powder and lipstick.

12:59. No time for that. It was showtime, and for the next few months when it came to events at the Point,

Avery was the star. With that thought in mind, she turned her head too quickly and was painfully reminded of her jacked-up neck. Couldn't focus on that. Duty called. With the office assistant serving as Maggie's temporary taxi, Avery bypassed her office door and continued to the executive office lobby to greet her first solo client. Just before rounding the corner she replaced her pained grimace with a smile she hoped was somewhat convincing. She squared confident shoulders to meet, and she'd already determined successfully land, her first client for the Point.

"Good afternoon," she said to the broad shoulders of the well-built man looking out of the area's floor-to-ceiling windows at the perfectly landscaped, award-winning golf course—the jewel of the club.

The guest turned around. Avery knew immediately that she was in trouble. The same hazel-gray eyes darkened with anger that had seared into her following the accident, that had haunted both her sleep and waking hours since, were once again gazing upon her intently, infused with surprise and a hint of confusion.

"Avery?"

"Cayden Barker." Avery hid the fact that she'd been surprised shitless behind a casual chuckle and an outstretched hand. "We meet again, a bit less violently this time, I hope."

"What are you doing here?"

"I work here." Her eyes went to the bandage on his forehead. "How's that cut?"

"Healing." Cayden frowned, a look that Avery decided was quite delicious, as were the plump lips now telegraphing his displeasure. Not at all the train of thought she should be riding right now.

"My appointment is with Maggie Sutton. Are you her assistant?"

Avery handled what sounded like a pointed dig with calm features intact. "I am the assistant director of events for the Point. Ms. Sutton, the director, had an unexpected medical emergency."

"I hope she's okay."

"She will be—" Avery paused for effect "—in about three months."

Cayden's response was a raised brow.

"I'll explain in my office. Excuse me for a quick moment." Avery walked over to where the club's beautiful receptionist, Vanessa, was trying hard to appear uninterested in Cayden, though her smile and the way she batted her eyes at him gave her full away. And why did how the young woman acted grate on Avery's nerves? She couldn't have cared less that the receptionist flirted with Cayden.

Or could she?

"Someone from the temp agency will be coming by. If I'm still in this meeting, can you please see that they're taken care of until I'm finished?"

"Sure."

"Thanks." She returned to where Cayden was standing. "Are you ready?"

"I'm here, aren't I?"

Avery heard the slight chagrin in Cayden's voice, but ignored it. The question was rather benign. She may have appeared as cool as an Alaskan glacier but inside her nerves jangled, her head still pounded and the pain in her neck now ran down one arm. On top of that, she was just as shocked at seeing him as he was her, but the last thing she could do was to reveal her discomfort or show how his presence affected her.

"Right this way." She crossed the marble-tiled floors and entered a carpeted hallway, trying to walk as if she weren't a close candidate for an appearance in *The Walking Dead.* They reached the double doors leading to the event-planning offices. She bypassed Maggie's corner office and walked into her smaller one with a less-spectacular but still-impressive view of the club's meticulous lawns.

"How are you doing?" Cayden asked from behind her.

Avery turned her whole body to answer him. She had no choice. Her neck now refused all mental commands.

"I'm okay. Why do you ask?"

"You walk as though you're a little stiff, which wouldn't be at all surprising. Even in that tank you were driving—"

"Ha!" Avery gripped her neck. "Ow! Don't make me laugh."

"It was quite a collision. My new, customized car driven less than a month may be totaled. Trust me, there's nothing funny about what happened yesterday."

"Again, I'm very sorry. I wish there was something more I could do."

Cayden waved away her statement. "Cars can be replaced. I'll get over it."

She retrieved a tablet from her desk, then walked over to a table that sat in the corner and motioned for Cayden to take one of the two seats. "I'm not sure you knew, but Maggie is expecting her second child. She's gone into premature labor. That's why I'm handling this appointment and will be in charge of whatever you have in mind to take place here."

"Damn. It seems I can't get away from you."

Avery immediately caught attitude. Her brow raised in response to his nerve.

"Just kidding. I shouldn't have said that."

"I believe we rarely say things we don't mean, at least in part." Avery shifted to look at him directly. "Our meeting was turbulent, to say the least. I can somewhat understand your hostility but would hate for the club to suffer because of what happened. Nor would I want us to collaborate for whatever you're planning in a negative atmosphere. If you'd prefer to work with someone else, that can be arranged."

Said with confidence and utmost conviction, though Avery had no idea if that was actually possible or not. One thing she did know for sure. She wouldn't be disrespected.

Cayden's expression was unreadable as he stared at her. His gaze unnerved her. She dared her body to squirm.

"It's my turn to apologize," he said at last. "It's been a stressful week, a stressful few months actually. You're not deserving of my sarcasm. The accident is only partially to blame for my mood."

A brief nod of acknowledgment was her response.

"Let's start this meeting over." He held out his hand. "Good afternoon. I'm Cayden Barker."

Avery eyed his sizable hand, the long-tapered fingers and manicured nails. She'd observed his big feet yesterday, encased in black Italian loafers. Men with big hands and feet usually had big...

"I thought about you last night," he said, interrupting her contemplation. His voice sounded sexy even in its conversational tone. The comment dropped her mind right back into inappropriate thoughts, like what could be done with big things at night.

Her nipples instantly pebbled. "Oh?" She crossed her arms.

He mistook her action for one of defense, and hurriedly continued, "Not in a bad way. You look familiar, but I couldn't place where we would have met."

Yeah, probably because you've tried to erase your criminal past from memory.

She shifted, swallowed and offered a less damning description of their interaction. "PDS. We attended the same high school."

Avery braced for his reaction. Recalling the thinner, Beyonce-blonde Avery could very well elicit the Brittany connection. Mentioning her older sister, Lisa, definitely would. They'd likely have to deal with what happened sooner or later. Best to get it out of the way. But he'd have to bring it up.

"High school, wow. That was a lifetime ago."

"We rarely interacted. I was a freshman the year you graduated."

"Ah, okay. That makes not being able to place you feel a little bit better. Though it's not unlikely there are others I'd not recognize or remember. I kept in contact with very few people from those years."

"Did you attend college afterward?"

Cayden nodded, stretching his legs—those long, strong-looking, rideable limbs—in front of him, the stress from earlier leaving his face as he spoke.

"Northwestern. Graduated with a bachelor's in computer science."

"Are you working in that field?" She knew the answer but asked, anyway.

"Since I was fifteen years old, at Eddington Enterprise."

"With your friend Jake Eddington."

His eyes narrowed. "You seem to know a lot about me."

"Anyone who went to high school with you knows that you and Jake were always together and obviously the best of friends."

"You're right."

"Jake and Bake? Stars of the Panthers basketball team."

Cayden chuckled. "That's my dude."

"I can hardly remember seeing one of you without the other. How is he?"

"He's good."

"Is it an event for the company that brings you here?"

"No, although the family will participate. I'm interested in putting on a golf event for charity."

"Do you have a time frame in mind?"

"People from all over the country will be invited. A date surrounding a holiday would be nice."

"For next year?" Avery opened her tablet and clicked on the calendar.

"Oh, no. Definitely this year."

Avery jerked her head up and immediately regretted it. She grimaced as the pain shot down her back.

"Stiff neck?" Cayden was out of his seat in an instant and coming around to where she sat. "May I help you with that?"

"What?" She massaged her neck as his close proximity caused a totally different kind of pain. She hadn't had sex in a while and her last partner's performance barely counted.

"Being an athlete during most of my school days, I've had to massage a strained muscle or two."

"Oh, okay."

It was so not okay.

He rested his hand just below her neck. Those long fingers were as strong as she'd imagined, loosening the tight muscles in her neck and causing moisture in other places. She dropped her head as he positioned himself more fully behind her and employed his other hand.

"Did you see a doctor? You're really tight."

"Not yet," she managed, lowering her head and biting down on her lip to prevent a groan from escaping.

"That's it. Try to relax."

His hands moved to her shoulders in rhythmic, circular motions. He searched out tight spots and pressed down with his thumb. It hurt, but only for a second, until the pressure loosened the muscle and gave her relief. If he was half as good at making love as he was at massages...

Avery leaned forward to break their contact. "Thank you," she said, her voice sounding more breathless than she would have liked. "It feels better."

There was a slight, knowing smile as he sat back down.

"That really helped." She got up and walked to the Keurig combo that sat atop a glass tray on a long, wooden filing cabinet, just for something to do. "Are you sure I can't get you a cup of coffee, or tea?"

Or me, her cheesy mind insisted on thinking as Avery struggled to regain control.

"I'm good."

Yes, you are.

Avery didn't bother to admonish the thought. A truer one had never crossed her mind.

"From your reaction, I take it that the summer calendar is fairly full."

"The Point Country Club has one of the best courses in the country, some say rivaling Seminole in Florida or New York's Friar's Head. Definitely the best golf course in the Midwest. Summer is a very busy time, as you can imagine. We have events booked out for the next three years. I'm almost certain the holidays are taken."

Making and dressing her tea helped Avery regain a sense of feeling normal. She walked back over to the table with the scent of mint wafting around her, determined to stay in control.

"Either the Fourth of July or Labor Day would work for those I plan to invite. What would it take to get whatever is booked on those dates moved to another time?"

"Because they're usually scheduled so early out, moving an event is pretty much impossible."

"Nothing's impossible."

He'd said it quietly, almost to himself. Avery looked up to find those irresistible eyes boring into hers again, her body reacting despite her intentions. She returned her attention to the calendar, searching for the first available date. The sooner the event was planned and over, the sooner she could get this manly mass of walking temptation out of her life.

Three

Later that evening, when Cayden pulled up to the gates of the massive property simply called the Estates, belonging to the rich, powerful and influential Eddington family, he was still musing on his earlier interaction with one Avery Gray. For sure, she was a nice-looking woman. Not in the overdone, manipulated way of the models on magazine covers, or like the obviously pretty receptionist who'd slipped him her phone number after the meeting. Avery's allure was deeper, more intriguing. She was cordial and very professional. He could tell that when it came to event planning, she knew her stuff. Yet a part of her felt guarded, as though there was something that she held back, something that he wanted to discover and get to know. There was an attraction, subtle yet undeniable. Cayden knew Avery had felt it when he massaged her neck. He felt it now, just thinking about her.

After a swift security check that Cayden knew was done through AI, the gates opened. His rental hugged the winding roads that led to the Eddington mansion at the top of the hill. All these years later and the sight could still take his breath away. He'd visited Point du Sable since he was ten years old, had moved in with the Eddingtons when he was fifteen and began attending PDS College Prep High School. Being a popular athlete and especially being best friends with Jake, he quickly grew to know almost everyone in town. It puzzled him that Avery hadn't seemed more familiar. He chalked it up to her arriving on the scene during his senior year, easily one of the busiest and craziest years in his twenty-eight turns around the sun. That year, and for several after that, his attention had been elsewhere, and after what happened because of the woman who'd then held his attention, Cayden had purposely put those years behind him.

Cayden passed several guesthouses and crossed intersections of the blocks where Dwight and Maeve, the eldest Eddington siblings, lived in masterpiece homes. He reached the mansion's circular drive, continued around to the north wing's separate entrance and pulled up next to Jake's latest toy, a white-on-white Rolls-Royce Dawn that he'd just added to his collection. If the dealer couldn't revive his Porsche, maybe he'd add another couple hundred thousand to the budget and go for one of those.

After giving the Rolls-Royce a cursory inspection, Cayden continued to the door. It was rarely locked, and today was no different. Still, it wasn't wise to walk into a popular bachelor's pad without notice. He pushed it open and stuck his head inside. "Jake!"

The sound of a pulsating bass came from down the

long hallway toward the back of the house. "Jake, where you at?"

Just as Cayden crossed the two-story great room, with its massive paneless windows letting in the meticulously landscaped nature around them, he heard the sound of electronic doors opening. He reached the patio just as Jake stepped inside wearing tennis whites and wiping sweat with a towel. Jake tossed the towel on a nearby chair and began clapping his hands in time with the music.

"Dammit, who told you?"

Jake smiled, revealing two dimples and teeth that sparkled against his dark skin. "You know good news travels fast in this town."

"I thought you just flew back today."

"I did."

"And you already know? How long have you been home, five minutes?"

"Long enough to kick Derrick's ass in two games out of three." Jake walked over to a built-in bar, opened a minifridge and pulled out a beer. He held up one for Cayden, who nodded and followed him over and sat on a bar stool.

Almost seven years from the time of Jake reaching manhood and the Eddington ritual that came with turning twenty-one, Cayden still hadn't grown used to hearing Jake calling his father by his first name. He'd been instructed to do the same but for him Derrick was still mostly "Mr. Eddington."

"I don't understand why you play your father so hard. You know he's getting older, man. Give him a break."

"I'm giving him a break just like the ones he gave me as a young'un on the court. Zero. Zilch. Nada. None." He handed Cayden the frosty bottle, then held his up. "Congratulations on becoming a member of the Society, man."

"I'm not there yet."

"You will be."

"Let's not jinx it."

"Then here's to the nom, dude. Congrats on that."

They clinked bottles and took long swigs.

Jake leaned against the counter. "What are you doing as your probationary event?"

"A golf tournament."

"For charity, right?"

"Yep."

"When?"

"I'm hoping for the Fourth."

"At the Point? This year?" Cayden nodded while taking another sip. "Good luck with that. You do know how hard it is to book that course, right?"

"I have someone working with me that I believe will get it done."

"Who, Jesus?"

"Avery Gray."

Jake's brow creased. "Why does that name sound familiar?"

"She went to PDS Prep."

"Our class?"

"Three years behind us."

"She's booking events at the Point? What happened to Maggie?"

"Maternity leave."

"Oh."

"I told Avery that the event would pull in members of SOMA from all over the country."

"Did she grow up here? The Gray family I know doesn't have a daughter named Avery."

"I didn't ask." Cayden's phone rang. He held it up and showed Jake the face. "Looks like we talked her up."

He slid off the bar stool. "This is Cayden."

Walking over to the patio doors, he continued listening while pushing the button that allowed them to open. He smiled and looked back at Jake. "You've got good news? Talk to me."

Once outside, he tapped the speaker button.

"...husband is a member of the Society of Ma'at. When I mentioned that the event was a benefit being hosted by them, she made a few phone calls, then called me back just now. I can't believe the weekend became available."

"I told you nothing was impossible." Cayden found himself smiling, cheesing, as his boys would call it.

"Yes, you did. This time you were right. I knew you'd be excited and wanted to let you know right away."

"You sound excited, too."

"I am."

Cayden determined that he liked hearing Avery excited, and surprised himself by imagining other ways he could make that occur. This relationship was strictly business.

Someone needed to tell that to his dick.

He moved from the swimming pool surrounded by foliage to a nearby firepit and sat in one of four cushy chairs. "I appreciate that. What's the next step?"

"There are several. I'd like to schedule another appointment as soon as possible to discuss them with you."

"Okay."

"What about tomorrow?"

"I'll have to double-check my calendar but nothing immediately comes to mind."

"Right now my day is flexible, and this event is a priority. So why don't you check your schedule and call me back with a time that works best for you?"

"I can do that. Either me or my assistant, Keri, will call you back within the hour."

"Sounds good. I look forward to hearing from one of you."

"I look forward to our meeting."

Once again, Cayden was smiling as he ended the call. Something about the woman made him feel good. He didn't know why. Never one to lack for female companionship, and not seeking anything serious anytime soon, Cayden had never given much thought to the emotional side of his relationship with women. If he was attracted to someone and the feeling was mutual, he made clear his intentions, set the boundaries, secured protection and went about doing what grown folks did. Most of his dalliances were casual, a friends-with-benefits type of situation. That was largely due to his first-and-only serious relationship. It began during his senior year of high school and lasted off and on for five years. She was older. He was naive. The fallout cost him his heart for a very long time and almost ruined a career that had barely begun. Since then, he'd shied away from anything serious, anything requiring him to let down his guard. Perhaps after the event was over, Avery would be open to a casual, mutually satisfying situation. He wouldn't mind being her priority for a minute or two and finding out if the skin on the rest of her body was as soft as that on her neck.

After a quick check of his calendar and text to his assistant, he called Avery.

"Good evening, Avery Gray."

"Good evening, Avery. It's Cayden. How does meeting around nine in the morning sound?"

"Perfect. That would give me the rest of the day to start putting what we plan into motion."

"Good. I'll see you then."

Cayden bopped back inside with a pep in his step. Jake was standing where he'd left him, leaning against the counter. His scowling face slowed Cayden's pace and then stopped it all together.

"What's wrong, bro?"

Jake slowly stroked his five-o'clock shadow and answered without looking up. "I remembered why the name Avery Gray sounded familiar. She has an older sister named Lisa, who went to school with Dwight."

Cayden relaxed. "Don't tell me. Lisa used to date your brother."

Jake shook his head. Cayden tensed a bit. "Avery?"

"I don't think Dwight knew Avery. He knew Lisa, though." Jake looked at Cayden. "Lisa was good friends with Brittany. Best friends, in fact."

"You're bullshitting."

"Naw, man."

Cayden walked over and sat down heavily on a bar stool. "How is it that the person who might be handling one of the most important events of my life is connected to the woman who tried to destroy me?"

Jake shrugged. "Avery didn't mention anything about that?"

Cayden shook his head slowly. "Maybe she didn't know."

"Man, you can't be that naive. Everybody in the Point knew about what happened. Those two are sisters. She had to know. You've got to wonder why she didn't mention it."

"Maybe like me she's letting the past be the past."

"I hope you're right. Because the last thing you want is something that happened back then affect your present and future."

Cayden accepted another beer and mulled over Jake's revelation while his friend took a shower. Jake wanted to drive over to Chicago's South Side for a slab of greasy 'cue. Cayden agreed to go even though what he'd found out about Avery's close connection to Brittany had left him with little appetite. All he wanted right now were answers and information. His nine o'clock appointment with the Point's event director couldn't come soon enough.

Four

At Lisa's prodding, Avery went to the doctor. She'd suffered a severe form of whiplash, made worse by going untreated and her working long hours. The discomfort caused by strained ligaments and a bruised muscle had traveled down to her shoulders and upper back. The doctor had sternly prescribed the wearing of a neck and back brace continuously for at least seventy-two hours. Unfortunately, that couldn't happen. The plastic-and-foam outer-space-styled contraption she was in the process of removing didn't go well with the navy tunic pantsuit she'd paired with navy and cream-colored heels and pearls. She was preparing for a very important walk-through and had taken pains with her appearance. According to Maggie, this was an event she had to secure at all costs.

"A SOMA event is everything," Maggie had almost reverently whispered during a conversation when Avery mentioned the pinnacle organization among the business elite. "They raise millions of dollars for dozens of worthwhile causes and give away tons of scholarships every year. From what I hear, it's extremely difficult to get into that organization. They only allow in our society's best."

Then why is a criminal spearheading their event? That was the question Maggie's statement had brought up, though Avery kept it to herself.

A coworker entered the restroom. Avery took a final look in the mirror. The pantsuit emphasized assets while toning down flaws. Thanks to her hair stylist, Touché, her curls looked amazing. She smoothed a hand over her stomach, which fluttered almost every time she thought about Cayden. Her mind replayed how seductive his voice sounded when he told her he was looking forward to the meeting today.

She looked in the mirror. *So what?*

Avery shook away the thought and immediately regretted it. A pain shot from the nape of her neck down her spine. She gritted her teeth against the pain, reached for the neck brace sitting on the counter and headed toward the door. The doctor had prescribed pain medication but while speaking with Cayden she wanted a clear head. Squaring her shoulders, she gave herself a pep talk as she headed back to her office. Each statement was punctuated by the sound of her stiletto heels clicking against the marbled hallway flooring.

Calm down. This isn't your first rodeo.

Cayden is just another Point Country Club client. You are great at this job.

You deserve to be here. Avery, you've got this!

By the time she sat at her desk, Avery had convinced herself that all of the above was true. She'd also resolved something else that bothered her—knowing Brittany. There was no reason to mention the connection. He hadn't brought it up, which was understandable. She wouldn't, either.

The phone's intercom buzzed. "Avery?"

"Yes, Charlotte."

"Mr. Barker is here for his nine o'clock meeting."

"Would you please escort him back? Thank you."

Avery calmed her nerves with a sip of tea, taking one last quick glance in a compact mirror before putting it away.

The door opened. Avery stood as Cayden entered, and walked around her desk to greet him. Her smile was genuine as she stretched out her hand.

"Good morning, Cayden!"

"It's morning," he replied, looking at her intently. He didn't shake her hand. "Not sure yet how good it is."

Avery dropped her arm. His mood switch took her aback. The carefree Romeo of yesterday had been replaced by the brooding bear she'd met at the crash.

"Did I do something to offend you?" A perfunctory question since they'd not yet sat down. "Or someone else who works here? The receptionist, perhaps?"

"Why didn't you tell me that you knew Brittany?"

Ah. There it was. The past she'd planned to ignore coming in and slapping her in the face.

Avery sighed. "This is a discussion probably best had sitting down." She headed over to the table they'd occupied yesterday without looking to see if he followed. He did, reluctantly, and only after she'd sat down.

"I assume there's nothing I can get you."

"Only the truth."

Sheesh! He's acting like I'm the one who embezzled money. Like I'm the thief!

Avery refused to feel intimidated. She sat back with a nonchalance she was nowhere near feeling and crossed her legs.

"I know Brittany. That's the truth."

"Why didn't you mention it, along with our high school connection?"

"My mind wasn't on what happened more than a decade ago. *Much.* Didn't think it was relevant to planning the event."

She watched Cayden's mental wheels turn as he digested that information.

"You do know about what happened, that Brittany tried to frame me."

Oh, that's your story?

What she kept in mind was the Point Country Club, and a client aligned with a prestigious organization wanting to produce a noteworthy, international news-making event. Businesses can't buy that kind of press. She kept her opinions to herself.

"I doubt there was anyone living here at that time who didn't hear about it."

Cayden's gaze was intense but she held it. Finally, he brushed a hand over his tight, soft-looking coils and let out a sigh.

"I guess I should be grateful that you didn't bring it up or judge me unfairly. When I found out that you knew her and hadn't mentioned it… I don't know… It… Never mind."

"As I said, it had nothing to do with the event we're planning. It wasn't my place." Avery reached for the tablet she'd set on the table earlier and clicked it on. "Speaking of, if we're done with that topic, can we discuss the golf tournament? Planning a large event like this can take more than a year. We've got just over two months."

Without waiting for a reply, Avery dove into the talking points she'd listed. "You mentioned guests flying in from out of town so I assume the event will cover multiple days?"

Cayden leaned forward, engaged. "Yes."

"A formal affair on Friday, fireworks after the tournament on Saturday and perhaps an inspirational Sunday brunch? How does that sound so far?"

"Sounds like my morning just got better."

Avery breathed an inward sigh of relief. She could almost smell the gunpowder from the bullet she dodged. The room's atmosphere lightened. Cayden returned to the easygoing guy he'd been yesterday. It took less than thirty minutes to outline the weekend.

"I'll put together a PowerPoint detailing each night, with options and suggestions for the program's flow. Things like whether or not you'll want a speaker on Friday, or whether the music will be live, with a DJ or both. The tournament on Saturday can be listed individually or grouped into teams."

"Which is more popular?"

"Teams can be fun, especially for charity. Groups can be formed by region or profession, or length of time in the fraternity. It's also a great way for those who live in different states to catch up on each other's lives while walking the green."

"I like that idea."

"Good. Considering that the day is spent in what will probably be a very hot sun, I'm thinking Saturday night should be casual. An upscale, Chicago-themed menu

served in a way that guests don't have to remain seated
but can grab their Vienna beef dog, for instance, and
walk around. Perhaps casino-style games beneath several tents, or other board games such as chess. I also have
ideas for the wives, if they usually travel to the events
with their spouses."

"That's a good question." Cayden pulled out his phone
to leave himself a note. "I'll find out and let you know."

After wrapping up the basic logistics, Avery said,
"One final question before conducting the tour to show
you where each event will be held. Have you selected
the charity that will receive the weekend's proceeds?"

"Another great question, one I haven't had much time
to think about."

"I'm going to need that information as soon as possible. Once I have that we can order mock-ups for your
invitation's designs. Those should go out no later than
next week."

"This is all happening very quickly."

"When people are coming from out of town, we normally try to give them three months' notice. Getting the
invites out next week gives them almost two and a half."

"Thank you, Avery. You're obviously very good at
your job. It's making mine much easier."

Avery warmed at the praise, and the way his eyes softened when he spoke to her just now.

"It's my pleasure. I love planning for charity events
and hear only great things about the Society of Ma'at.
Their presence here will be a boost for the club and for
Point du Sable. If all of this gets executed as planned,
we'll both look good."

Avery conducted the grounds tour. Though he was
a longtime member and had been to the club countless

times, she was still able to share a few tidbits that Cayden didn't know. He listened attentively, asked the right questions and wasn't stingy with compliments. When they reached the country club entrance near valet parking, Avery reminded Cayden again about securing the charity information. This time he shook the hand she extended. The tight grasp combined with his dancing eyes and genuine smile warmed her nether lips.

He took a couple steps toward the valet stand before turning around. "Hey, Avery."

Avery slowly turned to face him. "Yes?"

"I was going to ask about your neck, but I can see it's still hurting. I can recommend an excellent chiropractor to help alleviate the pain."

"I'm taking care of it, but thanks."

The meeting had started out on a tenuous note but ended far better than Avery could have expected. She went into her office, redonned her neck and back brace and daydreamed about all the ways that Cayden Barker could make her feel better, too.

Five

Cayden left the swanky offices of Eddington Enterprise feeling good about life. Last year, he'd created a software program that changed how the company did business and had positively impacted their bottom line. For the past several months, he'd been working on a generic, expanded prototype that could benefit any business or individual working in financial services. His invention could revolutionize the industry and have global impact. Dwight Eddington, a company vice president, felt that since the initial idea had been developed for Eddington, the concept belonged to the company. Cayden had vigorously disagreed. He'd designed the software, brought it to the company and had developed the new generic prototype on his own dime and time. He'd shared his plans out of courtesy more than necessity. Dwight maintained his argument and added it would increase competition.

But earlier today Jake and his sister Maeve, also VPs, had reconsidered their earlier position and sided with him. He was one step closer to introducing a product to the marketplace that could potentially make him a very wealthy man.

Cayden reached the parking garage. His eyes automatically searched for the navy blue sports car that the insurance company had written off as a total loss. His two-year-old Range Rover was parked in his garage, but he'd opted to take advantage of his insurance policy's rental option to test other cars. He'd been sure about purchasing another Porsche 911 until he took a two-hour road trip in Jake's convertible Rolls-Royce Dawn. That car rode as quietly as a convent and drove like the wind. Arriving at his charity golf event in that kind of styling would make one helluva statement. Or he could lose his whole mind and get his dream car, a Bugatti. At the mere thought, his mentor Bob's voice arose in his ear.

If you're going to drive a million-dollar car, make sure that you're a billion-dollar man.

Cayden left the decision for another day and instead slid into a pearl white Audi Spyder and engaged the Bluetooth to call his mom.

"Hey, sweetie, how are you?"

"Better."

"Really? I've been worried about you. How is your rib healing, and that gash on your face?"

"It's all good."

"Meaning you haven't gone to the doctor. Honey, I told you that deep cut can leave a scar."

"That'll make me look even sexier, right?"

Tami chuckled before responding, "I can't reason with you."

"Hey, Mom. What's for dinner?"

"Why? Are you coming over?"

"Depends on what we're having."

"You'll have whatever I'm cooking."

"Sounds delicious. I'm on my way."

Cayden's expression was neutral as he pulled into Harold Washington Heights. It was real estate owned by the Eddington family's nemeses, the Kincaids, but he didn't hold that against her.

He pulled his car into Tami's guest parking slot and navigated the meandering sidewalk to her first-floor unit. The smells of grilled onions almost pulled him through the door before Tami opened it.

"Hi, hon." She held back flour-covered hands and leaned in for a kiss.

"The smell of whatever you're cooking is blanketing the area. Don't be surprised if neighbors start knocking on the door."

He followed his mother into the kitchen. "What are you making?"

"Smothered steak and onions, with mashed potatoes and peas."

"Can I help with anything?"

Tami turned to him and smiled. "Sure, you can do the rolls and make the salad. Wash your hands."

For the next several minutes it felt like old times, just Tami and Cayden, the way it had been before Tami married Harvey, who'd died last year. Casual chitchat punctuated the comfortable silence before dinner was ready, the table was set and they sat down to eat.

"So, how's work?" Cayden asked after basically inhaling one-third of his plate.

"So far, so good."

"What do you like most about it?"

Tami reached for her sweet tea and took a drink. "That it's a smaller hospital, more intimate. Everyone knows each other. It feels more like a team. Not that there wasn't some of that in Chicago but it's different here." She shrugged. "I don't know how to explain it. How is it at the Enterprise?"

"Challenging." He shared his excitement about his invention, and his frustration at Dwight dragging his feet. "Fortunately, I have a distraction."

"Oh?"

"I've been nominated to become a member of SOMA."

"That hoity-toity men's group?"

"That philanthropic, civic-minded fraternity of successful, community-oriented businessmen, yes. That one."

They both laughed.

"Stuff like that is more you than me. But if it's what you want, I'm happy."

"I'm organizing a charity event as part of my probation. A golf tournament that will be held at the Point Country Club during Fourth of July weekend."

"What's the charity?"

"I'm still trying to figure that out. I thought about choosing the Boys and Girls Club. But in a way I'd like the cause to benefit someone here in town."

"Most people here don't need charity, son."

"True."

"But if there was a way to match people in need with the top-of-the-line facilities that Point du Sable offers… that would be huge win-win."

"Are you thinking about the hospital?"

"I'm always thinking of helping to make sick people

well. Our cancer ward is one of the best in the country. The difference in the type of care is startling—the treatment given to a patient in a hospital like PDS Medical versus that received in facilities with less funding. It's a blessing to work there but it also shines a bright light on the haves and have-nots."

"How would we pair patients in need with the specialists at PDS?"

"I know of a few organizations that help cancer patients who are underinsured. One or more of them could provide names of those who qualify."

Cayden tossed the napkin he'd used onto his empty plate. "Then it's decided. Proceeds from the golf tournament will go toward helping them."

Tami squeezed Cayden's arm. "Son, that would be wonderful! I could contact some of my old colleagues who now work at government-funded clinics or hospitals with no specialized cancer care. Somehow connect them to PDS Medical higher-ups. I mean, I'm sure there are people more qualified than me to put it together, but I'd do whatever I can to help."

"Your involvement would mean everything."

"Then I'd be honored, Cayden. I'm so proud of you."

"Think nothing of it, Mom," Cayden said, finishing off his tea. "That's just how we hoity-toity brothers roll."

The next day, Cayden called Avery. "I've decided on a charity—Point du Sable Medical Center."

"Okay," was her one-word, drawn-out answer.

"I know what you're thinking. That the people who go there don't need our money. This would be set up for a type of referral program, bringing cancer patients who need specialized treatment but can't afford it to a ward with the newest technology and the most talented staff."

"Wow, when described that way the plan is very charitable. That type of difference could indeed be lifesaving. What a brilliant idea."

"I can't take the credit. My mom's a nurse. She planted the seed."

"Then kudos to your mom. That topic is a very personal one for me. My sister, Lisa, has been fighting cancer."

"I'm sorry to hear that, Avery. Is she better now?"

"Yes, thanks to the very treatment you mentioned."

"She was treated at PDS Medical?"

"She's being treated there now with a combination of chemotherapy and holistic modalities. Five more treatments and hopefully she'll be cancer-free."

"That's good news."

"Indeed. So, we can move forward with the invitations?"

"I need to run everything past my mentor, who'll probably involve the local board. I'll explain the urgency of getting a quick answer. Shouldn't take more than a day."

"In the meantime, I'll get our designer started. She can create a placeholder. When the charity information is finalized it can be quickly inserted."

"You're new at the Point but this is obviously not your first ball game. Mind if I asked where you worked before?"

"Not at all. I was the director of events for Lake Chalet on—"

"Lake Shore Drive. I've been there a few times, no doubt at one of your events."

"Quite possibly."

There was a lull in conversation. Cayden found himself not wanting to hang up the phone.

"I have another call coming in, Cayden. I'll send over the invitation mock-ups as soon as I get them."

Cayden reached for the office phone to have his assistant, Keri, bring him a coffee, then changed his mind and headed to the break room for his choice of fancier selections. He settled on a mocha latte espresso and, shutting out what would be his mother's nagging, reached for a gooey sugar-laden donut. "You know the best part of the donut?" his mother would ask him, always concerned for the health of her fast-growing son. They'd answer together. "The hole."

He smiled at the thought, then bit off a third of the saccharin delight and washed it down with the steaming brew. Within minutes of returning from the break room, he was immersed in work—checking snail mail and emails and reading reports. Every now and then his mind would drift to the golf event being planned, and the talented woman helping him plan it. His loins tightened just as someone knocked at his opened door. It was a rare moment when he welcomed an interruption while working. Now, however, was one of those times.

"What's up, Jake?"

"You, man. That presentation on your software was stellar. You've impressed Derrick. That's hard to do."

"Your dad read the PowerPoint?"

"Not yet. I gave him a recap. I'm sure you'll be hearing from him."

"That's good to hear. Your dad has always been there for me."

Jake nodded. "For all of us."

"All I have to do is get Reign to marry me and I'm all in the family!"

"Oh, boy. Here we go."

"You know I'm not serious. I love your sister but Reign is way too—how to put this nicely—ethereal for me."

"You mean flighty," Jake deadpanned before adopting Reign's voice. "It's all about energy, frequency and vibration."

"Ha! You sound just like her, man!"

Jake reached over and picked up a piece of paper from Cayden's desk. "What's this?"

"A preliminary mock-up of the golf tournament invitations. Avery just sent it over."

"I like it."

"She sent several. I printed that one because it's my favorite."

"How's it going with Lisa's sister?"

"That event is my smoothest-running project right now."

"Did you ever confront her about knowing Brittany?"

"Yep." Cayden relayed their brief conversation. "She felt what happened in the past should stay there. I agree."

"Your voice changed. Are you feeling her?"

"Not really."

"Cool, bro. I totally get that answer. You'll be in those panties as soon as the Fourth weekend is done."

"Not so. I'm a gentleman."

Jake gave him a look.

"Okay, not unless I'm invited."

Jake cracked up and held up a fist bump. "My man."

Cayden had been joking when he said it. But it was actually how he felt.

Six

Avery loved food but had to admit that the intermittent fasting she'd read about and tried over the past week was worth missing a burger or two. Not only did the cream-colored suit dress she wore fit a bit less snugly, but she felt prettier, and more confident, too. Good thing, since she was getting ready to have lunch with her heartthrob—darn it, client—in about five minutes. Thankfully, at the last checkup, her doctor had given her a clean bill of health and cleared her from having to wear the neck/back brace get-up. Didn't mean she'd turn down a chance for Cayden to rub her neck, or other sensitive places. She was trying to think about him only in professional terms. But she had to admit, if only to herself, that the man had magic fingers. She thought this as she rounded the corner into the executive lobby and looked directly into Cayden's handsome face.

Could a Black girl blush?

As warm as she felt, Avery knew her body was giving the concept a good Girl Scout try. She covered her discomfort with a smile, reaching out her hand as she neared him.

"Hello, Cayden." They shook hands. "Good to see you again."

"No one turns down a chance to enjoy a good chef's handiwork. Once you told me lunch was involved, my acceptance was guaranteed."

"There's a hot new chef in demand all over the world. Maggie said he was the only one to do this event. I tracked him down in Switzerland and flew him in last night."

"Your brought someone over from Europe?"

Avery laughed and looked at him coyly. "Anything for SOMA."

"Ah." Cayden grabbed his heart. "I thought you were going to say anything for me."

Avery had no response for that. While walking the short distance from the executive offices to the restaurant located in the main building, they continued to chat about the chef, Lamar Princeton, and his innovative takes on traditional cuisine.

Avery paused as Cayden opened the door. "I hope you're hungry. I asked Lamar to prepare a sampler platter of items I feel will work well for your dinner."

"That's perfect. I'm starved."

Cayden placed a hand at the small of her back, a gentlemanly gesture made totally erotic by the words that accompanied it, the way they were delivered and the curious look he gave Avery when he said them.

The hostess looked up as Avery entered the room. Her

smile was perfunctory but widened considerably when Cayden stepped in behind her.

"Good afternoon, Ms. Gray," she said to Avery with eyes on Cayden.

"Hello."

She cocked her head slightly and looked up at Cayden with doe-like eyes. "Good afternoon, sir."

"Good afternoon."

Avery was not amused and wouldn't give the marginally rude young lady what she so obviously wanted—an introduction.

The hostess picked up two menus and stepped from behind the stand.

"We don't need a table," Avery informed her. They continued past the main dining room and down a hall of small, private dining spaces. Ornate doors held silver placards naming the rooms. Backswing. Nine Iron. Fairway. Eagle. Grand Slam.

She turned to Cayden. "Do you always get that reaction?"

"What reaction?" He looked genuinely surprised.

"Adoration."

"She's the hostess. It's her job to be friendly."

Cayden saw friendly, Avery saw fawning. Instead of pointing that out, she decided to stay focused on why they were there. "I decided to spare the chef and prevent an uproar by having our tasting in one of the private parlors. If those dining saw what we're about to experience, it might become a problem."

"He's really that good, huh?"

"I've never personally tasted his cooking but those who have give him high praise."

They reached a door with the word *ACE* stenciled on a platinum placard. Avery reached for the door handle.

Cayden reached beyond her and grasped it. "Allow me."

"Thank you."

Inside, a table for two had been set next to a window that overlooked one of several courtyards. Shade-covered stone benches circled a fountain spurting arcs of glistening streams of water around a statue of the founder of Chicago and the town's namesake, Jean Baptiste Point du Sable. A profusion of riotous colors framed the setting, courtesy of azaleas, columbine, yarrow, daylilies and peonies. Butterflies flittered and drifted about. The dining space was equally impressive. Meticulously shined silver and Bernardaud china set atop stark white linen. A crystal pitcher of lime and cucumber water was placed next to the small floral bouquet in the table's center. A bottle of something sparkly chilled in a crystal and silver ice bucket on a nearby stand. Though the room was brightly lit by both inside lights and outside sun, Avery thought the scene much too romantic. Was it her imagination or had the room become smaller, warmer and cozier? It didn't feel at all this way when she'd selected it yesterday afternoon.

While she walked over to the table caught up in these thoughts, Cayden took a turn around the room. He stopped at a picture that hung above the fireplace of a famous retired basketball star turned golf fanatic poised in full swing.

"Was that picture taken here?"

Avery nodded as she walked over to join him by the large, gilded frame. "This shot was taken before he hit a hole in one, on the tenth hole, I believe."

"That must have happened before I moved here."

"You're not from here?" Avery assumed that like the Eddington siblings, Point du Sable was where Cayden had been born and raised.

"I was born in Chicago. Moved here when I was fifteen."

Avery noted the tightness that formed around his mouth before he quickly moved to the table. She followed, her curiosity more than piqued about the story surrounding that move. Before she had a chance to question him further, the door opened and Chef Lamar Princeton walked in bearing a small domed platter.

"Hello!" Lamar's presence was as big as his voice. He was tall, at least six feet, and muscular, with long, tamed locs secured by a leather band at the nape of his neck. He wore black jeans, a white chef's jacket, a small silver-hooped earring and a winning smile. Placing down the platter with a flourish, he lifted Avery's hand and kissed it as he performed a short bow. "Ms. Gray."

Avery smiled at his antics and dipped for the briefest of curtsies. "Chef Lamar."

The chef turned to Cayden. "Lamar Princeton."

Was it Avery's imagination or had the brother just added bass to his voice?

Cayden shook the hand Lamar offered. "Cayden Barker."

Avery thought their handshake resembled death grips. Inwardly, she chuckled. *What do we have here? A little manly competitiveness?* She couldn't imagine what either of the other would have to feel competitive about. Must be a testosterone thing.

She stepped to her chair. Lamar was there in an instant, pulling it out for her. "You look lovely today, Ms. Gray. I like what you did to your hair."

Avery was impressed that he'd noticed. She reached up and touched the flat-ironed style Touché had suggested and was glad she'd taken his advice while at the salon and gotten lashes, too. She looked over at Cayden, who was again tight-lipped. Was he still reliving whatever memory her question about his upbringing had conjured up?

"What is beneath this dome that smells so delicious?"

"Glad you asked, Ms. Gray."

"You really can call me Avery, Chef Princeton."

"Only if you call me Lamar."

Lamar was actually flirting with her. There was no mistaking it now. Subtly, so as not to be disrespectful. But Avery knew a come-on when she felt one. The creased brow that accompanied Cayden's tight lips suggested he'd peeped Lamar's game, too.

"These are a few appetizers I'm testing, all with somewhat of a nod to Chicago. Warm pretzel balls with soft cheese fillings. Barbecued lamb pops. Savory, spiced buttermilk donut holes. Peking duck on cheese toast rounds."

"Goodness! My mouth is watering already."

"Then please." Lamar reached for the pitcher and filled each goblet. "May you enjoy these delicacies while I prepare the first course." He bowed again. "Bon appétit."

Both Cayden and Avery watched his exit. Cayden reached for his napkin. "He's full of bull."

Avery secured her napkin on her lap and gestured toward the platter. "Let's hope he's as talented as he is charming. You first."

Cayden studied the platter briefly before selecting a lamb pop. Avery picked up a pretzel ball, popped it in her mouth and groaned. "Oh. My. Goodness," she said while chewing, not at all embarrassed that she spoke as she ate. "Those are divine. Your guests are going to love them."

Cayden said nothing as he reached for a ball. He chewed slowly, thoughtfully, before lifting the napkin to wipe flecks of Himalayan rock salt from his mouth.

"Well…what do you think?"

Instead of answering, he tasted the duck on cheese toast. Finally, he sat back and smiled. "I think the dude can cook his ass off."

Avery laughed out loud. "I think I agree."

While sampling some of the best food Avery had ever tasted, she updated Cayden on the event preparation and got his final choice and approval on the guest invitations. Conversation quickly took a back seat whenever Lamar entered the room. Freshly cased beef, pork and plant-based hot dogs were boiled, seared in white truffle and avocado oil and topped with everything from crème fraîche and caviar to triple-cured maple bacon and shaved white truffles. Even the standard Chicago wiener was upgraded with Louis XIII cognac-infused mustard, heirloom ketchup, Vidalia onions caramelized in Dom Pérignon and a fresh herbed cucumber relish. A focaccia-inspired dough held deep-dish pizzas boasting six-different cheeses, white, pesto and tomato sauces and a variety of gourmet topping offerings—lobster, oysters, black and white truffles, Iberian-cured ham, saffron, foie gras and more. Italian beef sandwiches and hamburgers were made from Breedlove beef, an organic, grass-fed Wagyu variety from a ranch in Nevada that had been recently named "best beef" by the highly respected industry publication *Gourmet Dining*. Each sandwich was drizzled with Purple Stripe garlic aioli paired with an aged balsamic vinaigrette, topped with wasabi root and pink lettuce, then sprinkled with fourteen-karat edible gold. Lamar's baby back ribs fell off the bone and the side dishes were nothing short of spectacular. Just when neither Avery nor Cayden thought they could eat another bite, Lamar brought in the dessert samplings—sweet and spicy donuts, apple crumble, gold-dusted caramel popcorn, and minishakes made with chocolate, vanilla or strawberry gelato.

"How was your dining experience?" The smile that accompanied the question suggested that Lamar knew exactly how his diners felt about the meal.

"Chef Lamar," Avery began after washing down her last bite of popcorn with a sip of nonalcoholic champagne. "The reputation of stellar cooking that proceeds you does not do justice to the food I just ate."

"What about you, sir?"

Cayden leaned back in his chair. "I've never tasted food this good in my life. Where is your restaurant?"

"Currently I'm helping out a friend in Geneva. When stateside, I'm a private chef and caterer."

"Then have your calendar and business cards handy," Avery said. "Once the dinner guests taste your food, you're going to be a very busy man."

Lamar left the room. Cayden looked at his watch. "If I don't leave now, I'll be late for a meeting. But really, all I want to do is take a nap."

"I hear you." Avery stood. So did Cayden. They headed toward the door. "I take it the dinner menu meets your approval?"

"Everything you've done so far meets my approval."

"Thank you," Avery said softly, feeling all girlie inside.

They reached the valet stand near the country club entrance. Avery held out her hand.

"After a meal like the one you just served me, a handshake seems inadequate. That meal deserves a hug!" Cayden held up his arms. "May I?"

"Sure." She stepped into his light embrace. His hard body, strong arms and spicy cologne assailed all of her senses. She felt like a seventeenth-century maiden about to swoon, and quickly ended contact before that actually happened.

"Please have your assistant send over the mailing list. The invitations will go out next week."

"Sounds good. When is our next meeting?"

Avery thought for a moment. "For now, I think everything else regarding the weekend can be handled over the phone or online. Now that I have your preferred color scheme, I'll reach out to the company designing the ballroom and providing the tent and party setup for Saturday night, and will keep you in the loop with drawings, photos and 3D mock-ups. Once we've set up the ballroom, a day or two before the formal dinner, I'll invite you by for a final walk-through."

"All right." Cayden's expression was unreadable as he eyed her for a moment. "I guess I'll see you then."

"Yes. See you then."

Avery watched Cayden's retreating frame, admiring his broad shoulders, hard tush and his swagger-filled stride. He turned and, if not for a quick spin on her own heels, would have caught her straight-up gawking. Her mind issued a strong warning as she walked back to her office.

Careful with your heart, Avery.

She knew she would do well to heed the advice. Let her guard down around a man like Cayden Barker, and she could find herself falling in love.

Seven

When the weekend rolled around, Cayden was more than ready for a couple days to relax. He'd worked long hours on a detailed financial analysis regarding AI Interface, his industry-transforming financial software, and sent copies to Dwight and Derrick. With as often as his thoughts had drifted to Avery and what may or not have taken place between her and the chef, it's a wonder he got it done.

Once again, Cayden was enjoying the luxury of Jake's Rolls-Royce Dawn. Riding into the city had been nothing short of amazing while listening to music on a system that couldn't have sounded better had the performance been live. Even with the top down, the notes seemed to wrap themselves around him. The music and the wind made for little conversation. That was cool with Cayden. Between his software program and the charity event, he had a lot on his mind. Including Avery. She seemed almost as invested in the event as he was, and just as determined to make it a success. Probably because he was the first client she'd handled without Maggie, but Cayden liked to believe it was a little bit due to his swagger, too. She was digging him. As much as she tried to hide it, he knew that for sure. Admitting that he was equally attracted to her didn't come as easy. Even if he'd wanted to pursue something more personal, she was not the person with whom to do it and now was not the time. Eddington Enterprise. His interface invention. The fraternity nomination. All major, and enough on his plate. Anything or anyone else was a distraction, especially someone who worked at the country club, a place that was the social heartbeat of Point du Sable. What if a casual dalliance turned into her wanting something more? How easy would it be to navigate a scorned ex working at the town's most prestigious location? Tricky at best; messy on the worst side. The town was already so small that everyone thought they knew your business. Best to keep his out of the town's most popular social scene. In a very real way, his future and what it would look like was very much at stake.

They pulled up to the front of the hotel. All eyes were immediately on them as they uncoiled six-feet-plus of mouthwatering manliness from Jake's stark white convertible and headed inside Chicago's Four Seasons to attend First Friday, a Chicago-styled reworking of this popular networking model created exclusively for the crème de la crème of the Windy City's up-and-coming world changers. The games began as soon as they entered and crossed the hotel's lobby.

"Hey, handsome."

"Well, hello there!"

"Can I go with you?"

Both men were cordial, smiling as they responded, giving the women heart palpitations with a wink or two. They reached the elevator without being attacked, which had not at all been a certainty.

The door opened. Cayden was the first to step inside, leaning against the gleaming back wall. "I don't know how I let you talk me into this."

"Get used to it. Once you become SOMA…"

"It's a secret organization. Who will even know?"

Jake gave him a look. "You know better than that. The membership isn't a secret. It's what we do, how we move and the codes by which we operate that only insiders know."

Cayden's eyes slid toward his friend. "What do you mean?"

"Ha! Good try, man." Jake laughed at his friend's antics. "You're close to being able to know but not quite there yet."

They arrived at the ballroom where a long rectangular table held several computers. Behind them, hosts were checking off the heavily guarded and inspected list of invited guests.

"Jake and Bake!"

Cayden and Jake turned to see one of their high school friends coming from behind the table.

"Claude Long." Cayden grasped Claude's outstretched hand and ended the greeting with a shoulder bump. "Hearing that greeting, I knew it had to be someone old."

"I haven't heard that in years," Jake added, greeting their old friend, as well.

"Jake and Bake," Claude repeated. "That's how y'all rolled back in the day. Always together. Rare to see you at one of these," he continued with Cayden as a woman sidled up to Jake and he waved a goodbye to the guys. "Who let you out of Point?"

"I get out now and again. You still living here in the city?"

"And loving every minute of it. Chi till I die. There's nothing I miss about that soap opera on a hill known as Point du Sable. You still working with the fam?"

Claude nodded toward the direction Jake had walked but Cayden didn't see him. His attention had been pulled to the sight of a sexy vixen entering the room. Avery dressed conservative at the country club but seeing her now in a white baby-doll dress that hit midthigh, revealing lusciously thick thighs and a perfectly round backside further accented by strappy stilettoes, proved that she wasn't monolithic. The woman had a less buttoned-up, more playful side that Cayden immediately felt compelled to inspect more closely.

"...tried to get a job over there but... Cayden! Are you listening?"

"Sorry, Claude, but no, I'm not." Cayden extended his hand toward Claude without taking his eyes off Avery. "Good seeing you, man."

Claude chuckled as he shook it. "Unless you have an eye on your cheekbone, you're not seeing me at all."

Avery entered the crowded ballroom. Cayden quickened his pace, working not to lose sight of her in the sea of white worn by most First Friday attendees. He didn't question why he was following her and ignoring the flirtatious eyes and greetings of some of the women he passed. There was something comforting about seeing Avery's familiar face in the midst of strangers. Many who met him assumed him to be like the gregarious, extroverted alpha males he hung around. He could call up that persona when need be, but Cayden was much more comfortable in small gatherings of people he knew rather than large events like this.

"Cayden Barker!"

He frowned as his forward progress was interrupted by the woman who'd called his name now blocking his path. Unlike Avery, her face didn't look familiar.

"Um, hello." His eyes continued to search the room as he spoke.

The woman crossed her arms and cleared her throat. "Don't stand there acting like you don't remember me."

Cayden stopped looking for Avery to focus on the irritated—and irritating—woman in front of him. She was tall and wore a standout red dress that appeared to have been poured on a body that might have weighed a hundred pounds, one-ten tops.

"Teagan Howard, Northwestern. Professor Yancey's class. During an open test, I shared a calculator formula I created that saved your ass. How could you forget me after that?"

"Teagan! Of course, now I remember you."

"Yeah, after I triggered your memory." She ran her hand over long, black hair that neared her waist and made her pale skin even lighter. "It hasn't been that long."

"It's been a while." Cayden leaned over to receive the hug she offered. "How are you doing?"

"I'm good. You?"

"Working hard. Staying out of trouble." He resumed his search for Avery.

"What's the matter? You lose your wife in this crowd?"

Cayden smiled at Teagan's less-than-discreet try for

information. "I'm not married but I did see someone I need to speak with. It's good seeing you, though."

He started to walk away. Teagan fell into step beside him. "Not so fast, handsome. What's your number?"

Cayden gave her the number to his company cell phone.

"I'm going to call you. Let's do lunch."

"You take care," was Cayden's noncommittal answer before lengthening his stride to quickly put distance between them.

He reached an intersection in the ballroom where one could go left or right. He was just about to turn right when a movement to his left caught the corner of his eye. It was Avery, jerking away from a man's attention that was obviously unwanted. When the man turned and Cayden caught his side profile, he couldn't get to her fast enough.

"Avery."

"Cayden! Hi." The relief he heard in Avery's voice expanded his chest.

"Is everything all right here?"

"What's it to you?"

Cayden had purposely not acknowledged an Eddington nemesis and by default his, too—all-around-asshole Lawrence Kincaid. He placed a protective arm around Avery's waist—he'd analyze the move later—and continued to ignore him.

"I thought I saw you walk by. You okay?"

"I am now," Avery said in a low voice that only Cayden could hear.

"We're having a conversation," Lawrence growled. "And you're interrupting."

"Is that true?" Cayden asked Avery, still not looking at Lawrence.

"Yes, it's true," Lawrence said. "Now back off!"

Cayden looked down at the hand grabbing his arm and slowly up to its owner. "If you have any sort of fondness for those fingers, I'd suggest you unwrap them from my arm."

"Or what?" Lawrence took a step closer but removed his hand.

"No need to puff and bluff, brother. You're not worth an assault charge."

Lawrence broke out in a fake smile, straightening his suit and tie as he sneered at Cayden. "Yeah, you'd better back down. About to get in over your head, son."

Cayden returned his attention to Avery but kept Lawrence in his peripheral view. "May I get you a drink?"

"I'd like that."

They began walking toward the bar.

"Pretty big of you to sleep with a former enemy," Lawrence murmured as Cayden passed him. "You never were that street-smart, though. Must be hard up."

"What did he say?"

Cayden shrugged, pretending that he hadn't heard Lawrence. *Sleep with a former enemy?* The comment threw him. He tucked it away for later examination. For now, he tried to relax.

"Thanks for that interruption."

"No problem." He eased the arm that still held Avery's waist away from her and immediately felt the void. "What was that about, if you don't mind me asking?"

"It's business related." Cayden paused midstride before she expanded the explanation. "Something that Lawrence wanted held at the club that couldn't be accommodated."

Cayden didn't know whether or not he believed her

but he let it go. For now. They reached the bar. "What can I get you?"

"A glass of pinot noir, please."

They found a space at the crowded counter. Cayden placed his hand on the bar with a twenty tucked beneath it. The bartender saw it, nodded covertly and was over in seconds. He took their drink orders and brought over a bowl of mixed nuts before leaving again.

Avery bobbed her head to the beat as Mary J. Blige got the room "perculating." She leaned closer to Cayden's ear so she could be heard over the music. "I didn't know you came to these."

"I usually don't."

"I didn't remember ever seeing you at one before. What brings you out tonight?"

"Jake invited me, for one thing. Plus, with the event a month away I thought it would be good to see if there was anyone I missed or don't have contact info for who should be there. What about you?"

"I'm a regular. It's a great place to network so I guess you could say it's part of my job."

Cayden leaned away from her. His eyes twinkled during a head-to-toe scan. "I like your work outfit."

Avery laughed. "I said it's part of my job, not that I'm on the job."

"I was just giving you a compliment," he teased.

"Thank you."

The bartender brought Avery's wine and the bottle of imported beer that Cayden requested. He saw Jake approaching and waved him over.

"Jake, you remember Avery from high school. She's Lisa Gray's sister."

"She's Lisa Allen now," Avery interjected.

"I remember Lisa," Jake said. He extended a hand. "Nice seeing you."

"You, as well."

"How's Lisa?"

"She's had some health problems but is doing much better now."

"Your sister, Lisa. She's good friends with Brittany, right?"

Cayden looked at Jake with narrowed eyes. People shouldn't believe the hype. Men could be messy, too.

"They used to be friends. But that was a long time ago."

"What ended their friendship?"

"Brittany moved out of state. They lost contact and grew apart."

"Did you see Lawrence?" Cayden asked, abruptly changing the topic.

"No. He's here?"

"Yeah. I had to check him."

"What else is new. Just him or are the rest of the gang here, too?"

"Gang or gangsters?"

Jake chuckled at the reference to the Kincaid clan.

"I only saw him."

Jake shook his head. "I could do without seeing any of them."

Cayden knew why. Even though the families had never gotten along, the youngest sister, Priscilla, had tried to hook up with Jake for years. The bartender came over and took Jake's order. The DJ continued playing the hits. Bruno Mars came on. Avery grooved in her seat.

"Do you want to dance?"

"Me?" Avery asked.

"Well, I'm damn sure not asking Jake!"

Avery smiled as she slid off the bar stool. "Sure."

Cayden spoke to Jake. "See you later, bro."

"Nice seeing you, Jake," Avery added.

Soon the two were swept up in a sea of gyrating bodies. Cayden maintained a suave back-and-forth while checking out Avery's sexy moves. Her hips and booty making the flouncy dress come alive. *Damn, she looks good in that mini.* Had she lost weight? All too soon, the song ended. The DJ threw on a slow jam and switched up the party vibe. The opening notes to Ray J's "One Wish" changed energy between Cayden and Avery, too. He stepped close to her.

"I like that song."

Her eyes fluttered as she looked up at him. "Me, too."

Without another word he put a hand around her waist and pulled her into his embrace. A short gasp escaped her lips. She slid her arms around his neck. They swayed to the beat. She settled her body more firmly against him. He smiled, and had just begun to really groove when he felt eyes on him. He looked up. Lawrence wore a cocky, lopsided smile as he watched the two of them dancing.

Sleep with a former enemy. Must be hard up.

Cayden pulled his attention away from Lawrence and back to the voluptuous curves raising his body heat. His hand slid down to just above Avery's luscious backside, which very well could be the "business" Lawrence wanted but couldn't have. Floral perfume with citrus notes wafted up to his nostrils. Silky soft curls tickled his chin. He tuned into the lyrics about making a wish. No doubt, if he did that right now, Avery Gray would very much be a part of it.

Eight

The song ended. Avery unclasped her hands from around Cayden's neck. He didn't release her so she stayed in his arms, resting hers against them. The look in his eyes awakened her yoni and tightened her nipples. Another slow song began to play. Cayden pulled her close again and lowered his head. Hers raised as if of its own accord. Their lips were so close, almost touching. His hand traveled up her back, coming to rest against the nape of her neck. The gentle pressure of those long, strong fingers was all the encouragement needed. Their lips touched. Something inside her exploded. The music intensified while everyone in the room—heck, even the room itself—faded away. She felt his tongue swipe across hers, a silent invitation to deepen the kiss. She opened her mouth and welcomed him, a moan escaping even as his hand went from her back to her ass.

Avery couldn't believe how her body reacted. Every part of her combusted and longed for his touch. He kissed her lazily, thoroughly. She could have enjoyed those lips for hours, days, and wanted to introduce them to another set of hers. Lips that even now grew wet with the evidence of her attraction, her body preparing itself for what it clearly wanted. The feel of his shaft against her hard evidence that her feminine flower hadn't been that far ahead of the game. A part of her wanted to throw caution to the wind, pull him down to the shiny, hard floor and make love right then, right there, as people danced and networked around them. The other part of her remembered that this wasn't a house party. It was First Friday. With some of the city's most prominent movers and shakers in attendance. The thought caused her to step back so quickly that she almost tripped. Cayden's firm grip steadied her.

"I'm sorry but I need to…"

"Give me a second, baby. Let my body calm down."

At the mention and feel of his arousal, her whole body flushed. They continued to dance until the song ended and Cayden's soldier returned from "salute!" to "at ease." This time she stepped out of his embrace without daring to look into those eyes. Cayden seemed much less flustered. He took her hand and guided them through the still-crowded dance floor.

"Thank you. I enjoyed that," he murmured as they walked.

Avery couldn't think of anything to say. Right now it was a good thing that walking was a natural, automatic occurrence because she couldn't think at all!

They reached the edge of the dance floor. "Would you like another drink?"

Cayden seemed to remain unaffected, as though making out in the middle of a networking affair was totally normal and perfectly fine. He was still holding her hand, too. Everything about him felt good. Too good. That was a problem.

"No, thank you. I need to…go freshen up." Without another word Avery turned and made a beeline for anywhere Cayden wasn't. The bathroom, hallway, parking lot, any space with air and without him would do. She reached a bathroom and stepped inside. Thankfully, a stall was empty. She hurried into it, closed the door, then leaned back against the cool metal. Her nipples ached. Her pussy throbbed. *Avery, get it together!*

She sat down to handle her business, closed her eyes and took deep breaths. Slowly, her heartbeat and heated body parts returned to normal. At the counter, she ran cold water over her hands and wrists and dabbed some on her neck and forehead. Feeling back in control, she fluffed up the hair where Cayden's chin had rested, then pulled out a compact and lipstick.

A toilet flushed. A nearby door opened. The occupant sidled up to the sink next to Avery, openly eyeing Avery's reflection in the mirror while washing her hands. Avery put away the lipstick and reached for her powder brush. The woman walked over to an air machine, her eyes traveling several times to Avery while drying her hands. Avery's first reaction was annoyance. Who did this woman think she was to be checking her out? Then… another thought. She was the event director for a very prominent country club and had worked at Lake Chalet for two years before that. Perhaps the woman had attended a wedding at the hotel or had dinner at the Point. Perhaps they hadn't met at all but was rather a poten-

tial client she should get to know. This was a networking event after all. Clearly, Cayden's kiss still had her
somewhat affected. She put away her makeup bag and
pulled out her favorite fragrant lotion. When the woman
returned to the mirror and pulled out her lipstick, Avery
looked at her mirrored reflection, admired the red dress
on what had to be a size-zero body and smiled.

"I could never get away with wearing a dress like that.
Looks good on you."

"Thanks."

A rather dry response, but okay. Avery lotioned her
hands. "Nice gathering, huh?"

The woman paused to look at her, the tube of lipstick
near her mouth. "It's okay."

So much for networking. Avery didn't do women with
attitude. She replaced the cap on her lotion bottle, slipped
it into her purse and turned to leave.

"How do you know Cayden?"

Avery turned and replied pleasantly, "Cayden who?"

"Cayden Barker. Don't play dumb. I saw you two dancing."

The woman's demeanor was beginning to work Avery's nerves. She should have walked out of the bathroom
then, but curiosity and maybe just a tad of bitchiness kept
her glued to the spot. "Do you only dance with people
you know?"

"I might dance with a stranger," the woman glibly
answered. "But I usually don't put my tongue down the
throat of casual dance partners."

"You might want to try it. Could put some spice in
your life."

Avery managed to keep a smile in place as she exited
the bathroom. Inside she was feeling all sorts of ways. If

that woman saw her and Cayden kissing, there's no telling how many others saw the extended tongue tasting and what businesses or organizations those folk represented. Avery's professionalism was stellar, usually way above par. She honestly didn't know what had gotten into her to make her lose all common sense.

Liar. You do know.

She sure as heck did. Cayden Barker. Those eyes. His voice. That hard, chiseled body. Instead of turning left to go back into the ballroom, Avery turned right and made a beeline for the valet booth. She was sure there were people she needed to speak with, any number of potential clients who could bring business and good publicity to the Point Country Club. If that were the case, she'd have to catch them at another First Friday. Because if she ran into Cayden Barker, there was a real good chance that she'd kiss him again.

She was too keyed up to go home. It was one of the few times that she wished she had girlfriends. She could use a whole gaggle of women to distract her right now. But when their mother died and Lisa and Avery moved to their great-aunt's home in Point du Sable, Avery's bright personality dimmed. It wasn't until meeting Brittany that she felt real sisterhood with someone other than Lisa. She looked up to the woman, several years older, who was beautiful, confident, always the brightest light in the room. The day Brittany shared what Cayden had done, Avery had been appalled. She knew what betrayal felt like. Had dated a man for over a year before discovering that he'd lied about his marital status, then went to great lengths to hide the truth. It wasn't until her tablet ran out of juice and she grabbed his to check emails that she discovered that there was a very real wife and child one state over.

When the bank accused Cayden of theft, all hell broke loose. There were threats of charges and retribution. Words like *embezzlement* and *fraud* were tossed around like golf balls. Cayden was almost fired from Eddington Enterprise. It all played out on the front pages of the *Point du Sable Star*, and even made the news in Chicago. A few months later, it all went away—quickly, quietly, everything stopped. The threats were rescinded. No charges were filed. Cayden kept his job. Brittany left town and cut off all contact from her and Lisa. A hurtful act indeed. Later, she met a man who represented old money from Boston. They married a short time later.

Avery reached the city limits of Point du Sable. All the way there, she'd relived that kiss a hundred times. She wanted to experience a hundred more. Real. Up close and personal. Preferably while naked and lying horizontal. In a position involving numbers or cuddling after sex. It wasn't going to happen, the sex, but Avery allowed herself the fantasy, let her imagination run wild. The only place such intimacy would take place was in her mind. The Point had a strict rule regarding fraternization: don't do it. While interviewing, the club's zero tolerance policy was a point Maggie had underscored.

Then there was the matter that started it all. Or rather, the man—Lawrence Kincaid. She'd been caught off guard when he approached her and began flirting, asking, then demanding, that she give him a dance. She hadn't expected that. What had been even more surprising was when Cayden came along, swept her up as though it wasn't the first time and became her protector. She was taken aback not only that he'd done it, but how much she'd liked it. How being rescued made her feel. It had taken her a moment to even admit that was true. In this modern age of female empowerment, #MeToo and equality, admitting that a man stepping in to protect or defend felt good might come off as chauvinistic. Avery didn't care. Her dad had died when she was ten. She never knew or didn't remember either grandfather. There had never been a man in her life to come to her aid. Cayden had shown her how that felt. And she'd liked it.

What she didn't like was feeling embarrassed and a bit stupid for not being able to contain her "gratitude." Cayden was a client, the first event she was in charge of from beginning to end. That and the zero tolerance policy alone should have stopped her uncharacteristic behavior. That the event was for SOMA, one of the most prestigious organizations in the world, should have ended her shenanigans for sure. Instead of feeling as badly as she should about acting unprofessionally, Avery began thinking about how good it would feel to kiss him again. When her thoughts returned to the present, she found herself pulling into her sister's driveway. She hadn't thought about calling and hoped she was home. Lisa was a practical, no-nonsense kind of woman. Avery didn't know what she'd think about her making out with a client in the middle of the ballroom of a networking event, but she'd surely have an opinion and probably some pretty good advice.

Avery grabbed her purse and headed up the walkway. The stilettos that looked so cute an hour ago now felt like torture devices. She gingerly climbed the concrete steps and knocked on the door.

Her brother-in-law answered. "Hey, Avery. What brings you here?"

"I was in the neighborhood and decided to drop by?" Said in the form of a question and with a look of guilt on her face.

"Bullshit." His tone was gruff but his smile was genuine as he opened the door to welcome her inside. "Why are you limping?"

Avery reached the chair nearest the door, plopped down and eased her feet out of confinement.

Frank walked by, shaking his head. "I don't know why you women wear those stilts in the first place. Lisa! Your sister's here."

Avery knew the running footsteps she heard didn't belong to Lisa. She looked up as her niece, Amanda, bounded into the room.

"Aunt Avery!"

"Hey, girl." Avery laughed as Amanda fell into her arms.

"You look pretty, Aunt Avery. What are you doing all dressed up?"

"I left a party but am not quite ready to go home yet. Thought I would come visit you."

Amanda looked dubious. "You came here to visit me, or Mom?"

"Both of you, Miss Ask-Too-Many-Questions. How's Lisa doing?"

"I'm doing okay."

Lisa slowly entered the room. She looked tired, but her skin had gotten back some of its color. Her weight seemed to be holding, which gave Avery hope that the treatments were working.

"It's about time you came to see your sister."

Avery stood and gave her sister a heartfelt embrace. "I know, it's been a couple weeks."

"It's been a month!"

"No way!"

"The last time I saw you was the first of April, right before your boss went on maternity leave. I think it was the very next day you called and told me the doctor had put her on bed rest, and that you were handling the office on your own."

"Now I feel like a selfish cad."

"I didn't mean for that to happen."

"No, it should happen. I deserve it. I can't believe time is moving so fast. I'm sorry, Lisa, and promise to do better. You've got more color than the last time I saw you. Are the treatments helping you feel better?"

"The treatments make me feel like shit, but I think that means they're working."

"Mom, you said a bad word."

"How about another bad word—*grounding*—if you don't stay out of my conversation."

Amanda became überinterested in Avery's shoes. "Those are pretty, Aunt Avery. Can I try them on?"

"And break your neck?" Lisa asked. "We can't afford for two of us to be in the hospital. Go finish putting your toys away."

"But I want to talk with Aunt Avery!"

"I'll come help in a minute, honey. Let me speak with Lisa first."

Avery watched Amanda run out of the room. "She's growing up so quickly."

"She sure is, which is why you'd better get busy making her a cousin. Keep procrastinating and my child will be grown."

"I'm not sure I'm ready to start a family, but when I do, that process usually involves a man."

"You're still not dating anyone?"

"When have I had time? Maggie taking leave so early threw a wrench in all those social plans and hot dates that I didn't have."

The sisters laughed before sharing a few seconds of companionable silence. "Your boss have that baby yet?"

"No, but she went from semi to almost complete bed rest."

"How's work going, you being in charge of such an important location? It has to be a bit intimidating considering you've not been there that long."

"I've been too busy to feel intimated. There is a huge event happening on the Fourth that I only have two months to organize."

"Dang, why'd they wait so late?"

"I don't know, but it didn't matter. It's a charity for SOMA, the Society of Ma'at."

"The one with all those bougie brothers, attorneys, politicians and whatnot?"

Avery nodded. "They do really good work. There's even a connection with you, at least indirectly. The proceeds will help those who don't have insurance or can't afford it get quality cancer treatment at PDS Medical."

"I can't say anything bad about that." Lisa rose slowly out of her chair. "Come in here and tell me more about it while I make this chicken salad. Be careful not to get anything on that fancy schmancy dress."

Avery went to the sink to wash her hands. Lisa pulled items from the cabinets. "It's being put on by a guy who works at Eddington Enterprise."

"I should have known that they were involved."

"They'll probably attend but they're not a part of the planning. Cayden Barker is handling that."

Lisa whipped around. "Brittany's ex? The same one you crashed into a month ago?"

"Small world, huh?"

"What'd you do, offer him a discount for totaling his car?"

"His coming into the office was a complete coincidence, a meeting he'd planned with Maggie right before she left."

"That meeting had to be awkward."

Girl, you haven't heard awkward. Just wait. "We were both uncomfortable. I even offered to get someone else to take over the account."

"Doesn't sound like that happened."

"After learning about Maggie and we talked a bit, he calmed down."

"How does it feel working for someone you thought was a criminal with enough money and connections to make things go away?"

"I try not to think about that."

"Probably not too hard. He's a cute guy."

"I kissed him." Out. Just like that. She couldn't contain herself a moment longer.

The knife Lisa held hovered over the rotisserie chicken. "You did what?"

"Tonight. At First Friday."

Lisa eyed her curiously before saying, "Well, clearly you got over his transgression."

Her delivery had been drier than the Mojave Desert. Avery burst out laughing. The regret taking root in her heart dissipated the more she cracked up.

Lisa resumed cutting up meat. "How'd that happen?"

"The short version? I lost my frickin' mind."

Avery grabbed the bowl of onions and celery and

started chopping, a process slowed by drawn-out pauses while recounting certain key points and by her near-nonexistent kitchen skills.

"From everything I've seen of Cayden, he's a solidly good guy. I don't know what was going on back then to make him do what he did, but I can tell you one thing, Lisa, with no doubt in my mind. He's changed for the better."

"Sounds like you're crushing on him pretty hard. How does he feel about you?"

"I'll admit I'm attracted but there's nothing happening there. The two of us were just caught up in the moment. Another month and a half of working together and our contact will be over. He and I travel in completely different worlds. After the event on the Fourth of July I'll probably not see him again."

Nine

Cayden stood looking out of the large paneless windows that lined his office's back wall. Eddington Enterprise owned the town's tallest building, fifteen stories of glass, brick and steel brought together in a sleek, modern design that was as impressive as it was functional. The year following its completion, Stride Kincaid began boasting of plans to build a twenty-story structure. Derrick politicked and greased enough hands for the council to pass an ordinance that outlawed buildings that tall. That was one of many battles that had happened between the Eddingtons and Kincaids over the years. Cayden knew that Derrick had lost fights, too. But he seemed victorious in the ones that truly mattered.

For the most part, Cayden felt good, too. He'd put feelers out regarding his software and received enthusiastic responses. He'd also begun compiling names for a national sales team. There was only one area of his life that seemed out of sync. Him and Avery, and the distance between them. Professionally, there was no difference. She kept in regular, sometimes daily contact regarding every aspect of the event. The purple, silver and black combination matched the organization's colors, while the rich magenta accents alluded to THAT Pink, the charity organization that along with his mother and her team would oversee the project for PDS Medical. If everything went off the way it had been planned, this would be one of the best SOMA events he'd ever attended.

The event planning wasn't the problem. That all of the discussions in the past two weeks had happened via phone, text and email is why his world felt tilted off its axis. When she'd left for the restroom, and the evening passed without him seeing her again, he'd texted her. She'd responded and told him something had come up, and she was fine. He wanted to discuss what happened. The kiss and all of the feelings it had stirred up within him. How she felt about what had occurred and what she wanted to do about it. He also wanted to find out what happened between Avery and Teagan, who'd tracked him down and tried to grill him about matters that weren't her business. He'd shut down that conversation immediately, told her to lose his number and wished her well. With Avery, the situation wasn't so simple. The less they interacted, the more he wanted to be around her. On pure instinct, and before he gave himself time to think or change his mind, he tapped Avery's cell phone number and sent a text.

Are you busy on Memorial Day weekend? Would like to invite you to a party.

He sent a second text with the address and instructions to dress casually. Once done, only one thought came to mind. *That was stupid.*

A tap on the door drew him out of his musings and prevented him from sending Avery a third text telling her to ignore the first two. He turned to see another person who'd occupied his thoughts walking through the door.

"You wanted to see me?"

Derrick Eddington looked like walking success. Everything about him screamed money, authority, power, control. He was fifty-seven, but if not for the gray he allowed to streak his temples and goatee, he could have easily claimed forty or forty-five. He was tall, handsome, fit and self-assured in a way that went above simple confidence. His aura suggested he knew more, owned more and could do more than anyone else in the room, a trait he'd instilled in his children, and in Cayden, too.

"Mr. Eddington." Cayden paused as Derrick smiled. They'd gone past formal a long time ago but Cayden still preferred using the respectful title. "Thanks for coming over. I told Eileen that it wasn't urgent, that I could call you later."

"I needed a break from over there, anyway."

"Over there" was the side of the building holding all of the family offices. Derrick sat and stretched his long legs out in front of him. "Everybody arguing, wanting to be heard, changing their minds and getting their way."

"Well, if you thought you were about to get away from that," Cayden deadpanned, "you're sadly mistaken."

Derrick groaned even as his eyes smiled. "That damned Eddington energy has rubbed all the way off on you. I guess I have myself to blame for that. All right, lay it on me. What's going on?"

"I wanted to talk with you about AI Interface."

"Magnificent product, man. That presentation was spectacular."

Derrick's words tugged at Cayden's emotions and filled him with pride. Aside from his grandfather, who passed ten years ago, Cayden rarely had the praise of a father figure. Since meeting him at the Boys and Girls Club, Derrick Eddington had been the most constant example of what being a man meant.

"It's taken a lot of hard work but I'm confident that the generic model I've designed will change the world of financial services, especially wealth management. I also know how quickly the world of technology spins. The successful programmer isn't so much who has the best idea as it is the one who presents it first. That's why if the company is interested in first access to AI Interface, I'm hoping we can move forward quickly, within the next thirty days."

"You finally brought Dwight around? He's ready to sign off?"

"Dwight is my singular holdup, and if you don't mind me being frank, Mr. Eddington, it's starting to piss me off."

"Dwight has always been extremely cautious. You know that better than anyone."

"There's cautious and then there's contentious and foolish. Dwight has moved from the first to the latter. I don't want to engage in office politics and go over his head—"

"Isn't that what you're doing?"

"But if there's a window of opportunity to move forward, I'm not going to miss it."

"You two will have to work that out." Derrick's phone

pinged. He checked the face and stood. "I knew I was forgetting something."

"Another meeting?"

"Yes, with someone who's extremely important to my bottom line—my wife."

Cayden stood and walked around the desk. "Thanks for stopping by."

"No problem. We're looking forward to your event, by the way. Several of Mona's friends will be attending. Everyone is excited to be a part of what you've put together."

"I appreciate the support, Mr. Eddington. You've always had my back."

"I always will, son. We may not be blood but we're family."

Derrick's words meant more to Cayden than the elder Eddington could imagine. He hoped they still held if Dwight refused to change his mind and come around. Because regarding AI Interface, he'd like to have the family's approval. But with or without his boss's permission, Cayden was moving full speed ahead.

Ten

Avery battled with a band of balloons, two oversize, before finally getting them out of her back seat and securing the weight-laden strings around her wrist. She reached back in for a hot-pink gift bag and then balanced a customized ice-cream cake on both arms. After using her hip to close the car door, she tapped the fob to lock it and proceeded up the walk to Lisa's home. Amanda met her midway.

"Aunt Avery, let me help you."

"Thank you, baby. Can you grab the gift bag?"

"I'll take the cake."

"So it can end up an upside-down blob melting on this sidewalk?"

"Auntie! I won't drop it."

"I know." *Because you won't be carrying it*. "Here. I'm more comfortable with you taking the bag."

As they talked, one of Lisa's neighbors and good friends, Emily, came out and relieved Avery of the balloons she carried.

"Everyone's out back," she said over her shoulder as they reached the front door to Lisa and Frank's cozy home on the outskirts of Point du Sable. "Go on in," Emily said with a nod to the balloons. "This might take me a minute. I've made room in the freezer for the cake."

"Thanks, Em."

"My pleasure. She's going to love them."

"Aunt Avery, do you want me to put your gift over there with the others?" Amanda pointed to the dining room table laden with presents.

"Yes, honey. Thank you."

Avery continued into the kitchen, placed the cake in the freezer and continued through the back door to the decorated patio where a dozen or so people milled around or talked in small groups. She spotted Lisa and Frank sitting on a chaise and went over to join them.

"There's the party girl," she said, giving Lisa a heartfelt hug. "Hi, Frank."

"Hey there, Avery." Frank got up and gave Avery a one-armed squeeze. "Don't you look snazzy."

"You sure do," Lisa said. "I know this is a celebration but you didn't have to get all dressed up."

Avery looked down at the oversize top boasting bright pink flowers that she'd paired with white capri pants and black-and-white sandals, the umpteenth outfit she'd tried on before making up her mind.

"It's called dressy casual." Lisa looked her up and down. "What?"

"I'm trying to find the casual part."

Frank walked on the tiptoes of his Jordans. "It's country club chic."

Frank and Lisa enjoyed a chuckle. Avery missed the joke. Her sister's teasing had Avery questioning her choice once again, one of many questions she'd asked herself ever since accepting Cayden's invitation to attend a party. She'd immediately assumed it was an Eddington affair. The follow-up text about the dress being casual hadn't comforted her one bit. A casual outfit in Point du Sable's high society, country club circle could set a person back five figures.

Her first thought had been to turn down the offer. Getting Emily's call the following day about Lisa's celebration was the perfect excuse. Even though Lisa's party ended at five and Cayden's invite was for seven, celebrating the end of her sister's chemo treatments provided the escape she needed. In the end, she decided to put on her big-girl panties and go through with it. They still hadn't talked about what happened on the dance floor that night. Since she didn't want to spend the Fourth of July weekend with them dancing around an elephant, it was a conversation that needed to be had. Then there was that annoying part about her that had the nerve to miss the guy. Their communications were normally short and sweet, and often by text, but for the past two months they'd talked almost every day. She missed his voice, his easy banter, the subtle flirtation. She missed it all. As for the kiss, memories of that moment were still almost as strong as when it happened. A damn shame considering that was three weeks ago.

"I was teasing, kiddo." Frank gave her shoulder a playful punch. "Earth to Avery. Where'd you go, girl?"

Totally into the Cayden zone.

"Will!" Frank's attention had been drawn over Avery's shoulder.

"I'm sorry, what did you say?"

"Never mind. I need to go over and help my boy handle that grill. Make sure the barbecue doesn't become burn-a-cue."

Lisa's laugh turned to a gasp. "Wow! Look at that!"

Everyone turned. Emily danced her way over. The balloons bobbed behind her, the metallic material gleaming like crystals as they caught the sun. The oversize balloons spelling out *THAT Pink Lisa* were especially impressive.

"I know you're not really into the bling thing, but hey, it's a special occasion."

"I love them." Lisa gave Avery another hug. "That and the outfit? Really, sis, you shouldn't have."

Avery almost told Lisa about the invite from Cayden but right at that moment a couple of women from Lisa's job came over to admire the balloons and chat. Soon, the games started, drinks flowed and the food was laid out buffet-style. Emily made a big deal of announcing the end of Lisa's chemo treatments. The guests cheered. Avery cried. When asked to speak and then talking about how much she loved her sis, she came near to an all-out boohoo. Five o'clock came and went and the party continued. When Avery checked her watch she was shocked.

Six thirty? How'd that happen?

She walked over to where Lisa and Frank stood with Emily and her husband, Charles. "I've got to go, sis."

"I'll walk you out."

Avery hugged Frank and Emily and gave Charles a wave. The sisters held hands as they walked around the side of the house to Avery's car.

"Hot date?" Lisa asked when they got out of earshot.

"No."

"Yes," Lisa countered, using a finger to point out Avery's outfit. "Now it makes sense."

"No, really. It's work-related."

Lisa's voice lowered. "You're going to see him, aren't you?"

"Who?"

"Who, who?" Lisa mocked a hoot owl.

"I don't know what you're talking about." Avery pointed the fob toward her car and turned to hug Lisa. "Today was amazing. You look great. I'm so happy you're on the other side of that beast."

"There's still a ways to go before I'm declared cancer-free."

"I'm declaring it now." They hugged again. "Love you."

"Love you, too."

Avery opened her car door. Lisa turned to leave. "Have fun wherever you're going."

"I will."

"Tell Cayden I said hi."

Avery arrived in Chicago just before seven and texted Cayden that she was almost there. She'd engaged her GPS with the address he'd texted earlier. The closer the automated voice said she was to her destination, the more she felt she'd flubbed the address. She was nowhere near any of the zip codes she'd imagined the instructions would take her. By the time she pulled up to a nondescript brick apartment building with the announcement that "You have arrived," Avery was sure she'd messed up. She pulled out her phone and was just about to recheck the text when Cayden strolled out of the building.

The first thing she noticed? What he was wearing—

T-shirt, jeans, flip-flops. *Does that man actually have on flip-effing-flops?* As she looked down at her outfit, and the strappy sandals encasing her fresh pink pedicure, Frank walking on his tiptoes swam into memory. There was no way around it and no doubt about it. She was definitely overdressed.

Cayden reached her car. "Hi!"

Wishing for the clothes she had on before showering and changing, she reluctantly opened the door.

"You made it!"

Cayden hadn't noticed her complete and total discomfort. *Men!* He hugged her, and for a second, she was distracted from her fashion faux pas.

Stepping away he remarked, "You got the text that said casual, right?"

So much for being distracted. "I know," Avery snapped. "I'm overdressed."

"You look good, don't get me wrong. It's just that, well, you'll see."

They entered the building. Though well-maintained it was obviously old, with areas in need of repair. They passed through a lobby-like area with a counter that ran the length of one wall. Behind it were brightly decorated posters with positive sayings that showed laughing, older people enjoying various activities. On the other side of the lobby were two smaller rooms with what looked like an activity calendar attached to the wall between them. Tables and chairs were scattered about. A few held games or decks of cards. When they reached the elevator that led into a long hall, Avery saw a gray-haired woman using a walker and being assisted by a slightly younger woman walking beside her.

She turned to Cayden. "Who lives here?"

"A dear friend." Cayden's eyes laughed. Clearly, he noted and was enjoying her confusion. The elevator door opened. He ushered her inside and pushed the button for the top floor. Avery studied the posters taped to the elevator walls.

"Rising Star Assisted Living?"

"You got it, the name of this facility."

Facility?

Before she could ask further questions, they reached the tenth floor. The elevator doors opened. Straight ahead was a large, bright room filled with people. None looked under seventy years old. Colorful streamers crisscrossed the walls and ceiling. Silver food warmers lined several rectangular tables at the back of the room. At the front was a podium with a round cage filled with brightly colored balls.

"There's my cutie pie," a silver-haired lady exclaimed as she toddled up to Cayden and grabbed his arm. "I thought you'd run out on me."

Her gaze slid to Avery. "Who is this? Your sister?"

"No, Miss Kay. This is a very good friend, Avery Gray."

"Your girlfriend?" Her sweet face twisted into a frown. "You stepping out on me?"

"Never, Miss Kay. Avery, this is Miss Kay Morales. She was my fourth-grade teacher. I was insecure, introverted, didn't make friends easily. She suggested I join the Boys and Girls Club where she volunteered. It became my home away from home for several years and she became my best friend. She still is."

Kay's eyes shone as though she really believed him.

"I know he's lying," she said to Avery, dispelling the thought. "But it sure sounds good!" She linked an arm through Avery's as they entered the room together. "What's your name again, sweetie?"

"Avery, ma'am."

"She's very pretty, Cayden. If she isn't your girlfriend, she should be."

From the moment they entered the room, it was non-stop conversation. Little ladies pulled on Cayden. Sweet codgers winked at her. A man older than Jupiter pinched her butt. She was called a "looker" for the first time in her life. It took a moment to realize that beside the discarded plates of a recently eaten picnic fare, cards and chips were stacked in front of every seat at the tables. No. Couldn't be.

Bingo, Cayden? Seriously?

As serious as a lockdown in all fifty states. She'd barely digested that bit of news when once again Cayden's name was called.

"Come on, young man," said a spry senior wearing VFW regalia. "Let's get this party started!"

Cayden reached for her hand. "Come on!"

Next thing she knew, Avery had been given a two-minute drill on how to turn the cage and reach in for the balls. Cayden was the caller. Competition was fierce. "Bingo!" rang out all over the room, sometimes prematurely or flat-out wrong.

"Give it up!" one disgusted player shouted after a false alarm. "Myrtle, you're as blind as a bat!"

People clapped and cheered when their friends won but Cayden had to step in between two men who felt the other was cheating. Avery was called in to mediate. She double-checked the cards for accuracy as though it was a hopeful student's college entrance exam. Two hours flew by and then it was over. Avery had had the time of her life!

"How'd you like the party?" Cayden teased as they walked out into the warm night air.

"Who knew bingo could be so much fun?"

"Fun? I thought at any moment a riot could break out!"

"If Myrtle had gotten it wrong one more time, it may have!"

They cracked up all the way to Avery's car. "Where are you parked?"

"I'm around back."

"Thanks for inviting me here tonight. After all the stress of the job, it's just what I needed. I want to adopt your teacher, Miss Kay. That she's kept in touch with you all of these years is probably some kind of record."

"I was having a tough time when we met. Chaotic home life. Low self-esteem. She noticed and took special care. Now it's my pleasure to take care of her. That type of kindness is never forgotten."

A few seconds of silence passed. Cayden sighed and looked at the sky. Avery tried to think of a clever segue from fourth graders to first kisses.

"You know, Cayden—"

"It's such a beau—"

Cayden gestured to Avery. "You first."

"What were you going to say?"

"It's a beautiful night and I'm not ready to go home yet. There's a neighborhood bar not too far away. Can I buy you a drink?"

"Absolutely."

"Why don't you leave your car here? The neighborhood is safe, but I'd feel better if you were with me." When she still hesitated, he continued, "I promise to get you back before the clock strikes twelve and you have to roll home in a pumpkin."

"Well, in that case…"

Cayden and Avery walked down the street and around the corner. She was surprised when Cayden stopped in front of a black SUV.

"This is your car?"

He nodded as he opened her door. Once she was secure, he bopped around to his side of the car, jumped in and took off.

"Nothing against practical vehicles but there's a whole lot of distance between what you're now driving and the car in the accident. Did I scare you away from ever wanting to own something so costly again?"

"Hardly." He fiddled with the radio. "This is a rental. Easier to blend in. Driving a luxury car in these parts might put a target on your back."

"Come to think of it, I never asked what happened to your car. Were they able to fix it?"

"Completely totaled."

Avery's hand flew to her mouth.

"Don't worry. Insurance covered it. I ordered another one almost exactly like the one you hit."

A short time later, they pulled up to a building that looked as old as the one they'd just left. Jack's Joint flashed from a partially lit neon sign.

At Avery's raised brow, Cayden responded, "Don't judge a book by its cover."

Inside, Jack's Joint was all dark wood and burgundy leather, dim and cozy, the way one would imagine a "joint" to be. Blues notes greeted Avery like an old friend, though they'd never met before. A group of men at the bar eyed her appreciatively, while a couple more played pool in the back.

"Hey, Jack!" Cayden waved to the older, bald-headed man behind the bar.

"There's no women in here," Avery hissed.

"You're here, and you're with me," was Cayden's confident reply. He led them to one of only two booths, both positioned by a jukebox that looked to have been delivered around 1965.

"Pinot noir, same as always?"

That "always" had only been one drink one time was something Avery strongly considered pointing out. Instead, she simply nodded and watched how Cayden's ass blessed the hell out of those jeans as he made his way to the counter.

Don't forget why you agreed to this drink, she told herself, mentally preparing her dissertation. That ass she'd admired just moments before had barely touched leather when she went into the spiel.

"What happened on the dance floor that night shouldn't have happened."

"I know," Cayden quickly interjected before she could continue, calmly placing a napkin beneath the glass of wine he'd set in front of her. He sat back, a bottle of beer in hand. "That whole situation was way too public and, because of that, ended way too soon."

For a second, Avery was stunned speechless. Had she been expecting a comeback, which she hadn't, it would not have included anything of what he just said.

"I know that's not what you meant, but don't you want to at least have a sip of your wine before having—" air quotes "—the conversation?"

Avery took the briefest of sips before jumping right back into her speech. "Like I said…"

Her exaggerated attitude combined with a stiffly pointed finger and a perfectly executed neck roll had both of them bursting with laughter again.

"Girl, you were ready!"

"It did sound like I was in a rush to clear the air."

"I'll put it this way. If your words were a race, you'd have won Olympic gold."

Avery chuckled.

"Record-breaking, FloJo hair and nails in your face kind of winning race."

"It's not the easiest conversation. I guess I wanted to speak my mind before I changed it."

"Neither one of us had making out in mind when we stepped on the dance floor. It just happened."

"I know, and I couldn't have been more shocked. That type of behavior is totally not me. At a networking affair I'm attending in a professional capacity. With a client whose event I'm planning, in front of hundreds of other potential businesses that could be future clients? I was beyond embarrassed."

"Is embarrassment the 'something came up' scenario that you texted me?"

Avery nodded. "I already felt guilty about what happened and then was confronted in the bathroom. That was my exit cue."

"Her name is Teagan. I'm sorry about that."

"An ex still harboring feelings of possession?"

"A classmate who I barely know."

"Either way, I apologize for getting caught up in the moment."

Cayden eyed her briefly. "If I apologized, I'd be lying. I very much enjoyed what happened that night."

His words did things to Avery's insides. She squeezed her thighs together and sat straighter in the booth.

"I enjoyed it too, but it can't happen again."

"Okay."

"Intimate interactions with Point Country Club clients is not permitted."

"What about when those persons are no longer clients?"

Avery thought that a perfect moment to observe her surroundings and enjoy several slow sips of wine.

"I probably should get back," she said, putting down her still-unfinished glass.

"Tomorrow's Sunday. The night's just getting started."

"Not for me."

"All right, pretty lady. Let's go."

Cayden stood and reached for her hand. When their fingers touched, she ignored the jolt of blatant desire that arose from her core and swirled around her mouth. The ride back to her car was mostly silent. She tried to engage Cayden in conversation about his tournament, but golf was the last thing on either of their minds.

When they reached her car, Avery didn't wait for Cayden to open her door. In fact, the tires had barely stopped rolling when she engaged the handle.

"I had a great time tonight," she said sincerely.

"Me, too. Be safe."

"I'll have Charlotte send over the updated guest list, and the details that have been confirmed for Saturday night."

"Okay. Bye."

Avery's exit was stalled by a hand on her upper left

arm. When she turned to find out why he'd stopped her, his lips held the answer. They pressed against hers—hot, hungry—his tongue sliding into her open mouth like a baseballer sliding into home plate. Unable to think, Avery simply reacted. She angled her head as their tongues danced and dueled. His hand slid from her arm to her leg, a finger grazing the hardened nipple of a breast aching with need. Desire spread through her body like molten lava. For a touch she could never feel. For a love that could never be. She broke the kiss.

"Cayden." His name was an exhalation, the last breath of insanity.

He straightened. Gripped the steering wheel. Stared straight ahead. She nearly bolted from his car to the safety of her own, started it up and pulled off without a wave of goodbye. It was blocks before normal breathing resumed, miles before she'd convinced herself nipping whatever notions Cayden had about them in the bud was the right thing to do. That didn't mean it felt good.

Damn.

Eleven

For Chicago's upper crust, First Fridays were the thing. For the Eddingtons in Point du Sable, from as long as could be remembered, First Sundays at the Estates were the coveted invite. If you found yourself on the right side of luck, it was a gathering not to be missed. Cayden remembered the first time he'd attended a First Sunday with his new friend Jake, whose father, Derrick, was on the board and served as a mentor at the Chicago-area Boys and Girls Club where Cayden spent weekdays after school and almost every Saturday. Jake, also ten, had accompanied his father to a sporting event held at the center. The two had become fast friends. A few months later, Jake invited him over for what he'd described as "lunch." Cayden's life was forever changed. Upon arriving, he'd mistaken the house for a hotel. His family had always lived in apartments. He couldn't believe only one family lived in a structure that sat on five acres and spanned well over twenty thousand square feet. It was the beginning of many weekends spent at Jake Eddington's house. Years later trouble arrived by way of his mother's boyfriend turned husband—Cayden never considered him "step-father"—and Cayden's title at the estate changed from visitor to resident. A year after that he began working part-time at Eddington Enterprise, mostly acting as go-pher for the execs, while being slowly, almost casually, taught the science of money, the institution of finance and navigating the world of the elite from the bottom up.

Cayden was about to pull into the lot when he noticed a professionally dressed attendant heading his way.

"Good afternoon, sir." The well-groomed young man had close-cropped hair, piercing black eyes and teeth that gleamed against his smooth dark skin. "I'll be glad to park that baby for you." His slender fingers mirrored the car's sleek lines. "That's a pretty car."

"Never thought of it as a female," Cayden replied to the kid whose open admiration for the car, the way Cayden could see the young man imagining himself in one like it, somehow reminded him of his younger self. "But given the curves, I get where you're coming from."

Cayden turned toward the pathway leading from the garage to the main house, and around to the vast patio where the brunches had been held for the past five years. Strategically placed misters helped make cool the short walk on hot days such as this one, along with a thin can-opy shielded by leafy foliage and miniature white lights. No matter the weather, those who chose to dine inside enjoyed a solarium that boasted exotic plants from all seven continents, furniture covered in leather, suede, silks and linen, and some of the finest stone- and ironwork in the world. The food was exceptional, prepared by award-winning chefs often flown in specifically to cater the affair. It was a world that before meeting Jake, Cayden never knew existed. In moments like this, he still questioned whether or not he truly belonged there.

"Cayden! There you are."

"Hello, Monamama."

Mona Eddington, the undisputed matriarch of the Eddington clan and influential Point du Sable socialite, chuckled at the pet name Cayden had used since the age of ten. She held out diamond-laden arms and tossed air kisses on both sides of his face before folding him into her embrace. "I just asked Jake about you."

"Is everything okay?"

"Couldn't be better. In fact—" she hooked her arm in his, leaning toward him conspiratorially as they walked toward the raised table where the Eddingtons held court "—I hear you're poised to become a Society man."

"So much for secrecy during the vetting and voting process."

"Darling, nothing happens in this town that the Eddingtons don't know about. Surely, you've learned that by now."

Cayden chuckled. "Better than anyone."

"You know what that means, right?"

"What, that this increases the extent of your nosiness?"

Mona swatted him playfully. "Your becoming a part of the club raises your status and profile. Only ladies with specific qualities can breathe that rare air."

Cayden had an idea where this was going and wasn't sure he liked it.

"Your choice in partner will be extremely important.

She must be the right...pedigree...to move comfortably and correctly in these circles, one who can support and assist you where you need to go."

The duo strolled through the room. Cayden either spoke to or waved at the people he knew and felt curious stares from the people he didn't, all while processing what Mona had said. Just as he was going to ask for a deeper explanation of her partner comment, they reached the head table. He gave a general greeting to the group and received various responses. Along with the Eddington family—father Derrick, brothers Dwight and Jake, sisters Maeve and Reign—and a few other close relatives or associates was a strikingly beautiful woman Cayden was sure he'd never seen before. As Mona pulled him in that direction, the reason behind her comments became clear.

"Sit on this end," she instructed. "There's someone I'd like you to meet." He steeled himself for the encounter and hoped his lips were turned up at the ends.

"Delaney, this is Cayden Barker. Cayden, this is the beautiful daughter of a dear friend of mine, Delaney Witherspoon."

She held out her hand as a princess might. Like she expected him to kiss it, bow, then pledge allegiance to the king. In an awkward transition, he placed his hand beneath hers and guided them into a handshake. Cayden immediately knew that the action displeased her. Miss Kay, or any newborn, could have managed a firmer grip. He poured charm on his next words to make up for the slight.

"It is a pleasure to meet you, Delaney."

"Likewise."

Her voice was low and cultured, her movement restrained, with lips that barely moved when she spoke. He immediately thought of Avery's verbal antics.

Like I said...

A snicker flew out of his mouth.

Delaney recoiled. Mona's eyes narrowed. His attempt to turn the gaffe into a cough was pitiful at best. A meeting obviously important to Mona was going down like the *Titanic*. Cayden's movements were deliberate as he pulled back the chair and sat next to Delaney. Now was not the time to piss off Monamama. He reached for the water in front of him and took a recalibrating drink. When he spoke, the suave, confident businessman persona had been retrofitted and secured.

"That's a lovely name, Delaney." The compliment produced the merest hint of a smile. "What brings you to Point du Sable?"

Cayden didn't really care why she was in town, but the question produced conversation and eased the tension from Mona's face. He quickly learned that Delaney was the only—translated spoiled, pampered, doted upon—daughter of a prominent Washington, DC, judge and his US-ambassador-appointed wife. She spoke three languages, had traveled the world and was the creator and operator of several successful internet businesses that centered around her international commerce major.

"She graduated summa cum laude," Mona added. "Beauty and brains are a powerful combination. Whoever is fortunate enough to win this woman's hand will truly be unstoppable."

At the thought of offering up Jake or Dwight for that privilege, he almost snickered again.

"You have a very impressive résumé," Cayden offered instead, knowing he should have said more but feeling fresh out of quick wit. Everything about Delaney was superlative. He was just not interested.

"I shared with Delaney your nomination to the Society, and the event on the Fourth. Her dad, Reginald, is a third-generation member. Both he and his lovely wife, my friend Lorelei, will be at the golf tournament next month." Mona turned to Delaney. "His charity is PDS Medical, through an organization dedicated to fighting cancer called THAT Pink."

"Philanthropy is very necessary, and so important," Delaney cooed. She placed a soft hand on his wrist. "Tell me how you came upon that choice."

Back on familiar territory, Cayden relaxed as he shared news about his project. Brunch service began. Guests mingled. Conversation flowed as freely as the Goût de Diamants. When a clearly smitten company VP introduced himself to Delaney, Cayden used the opportunity to make a quick break. He saw Jake and went over for moral support.

"Did you survive Mom's matchmaking?" Jake asked before Cayden got a word out.

"Why didn't you warn me?"

"I didn't know. From what I understand, she only arrived this morning."

"Mona is championing her for a bride march. Why didn't she pair her with you or Dwight?"

"Man, Delaney is like our sister. We've known her all our lives."

"Why hadn't I met her?"

"By the time you moved here she was attending a boarding school in Europe. Mom and Lorelei usually scheduled their get-togethers on other continents."

"She'll be back on the Fourth." Cayden let out a sigh. "That's going to be tricky. I can already tell."

"You haven't heard tricky until you hear my news."

"What?"

"Brittany's back."

Cayden didn't respond.

"Don't trip on that, man. I've got good news, too. Dwight's ready to sign off on your software. AI Interface will belong solely to you."

"Cool."

"Is that all you can say? You're about to become a billionaire!"

Jake's news produced two responses—thrilled and terrified. Bob Masters had warned him to stay far away from scandal. But now with Delaney circling and Brittany back in town, it seemed trouble could very well come knocking at his door.

Twelve

June whizzed by. With special events happening every weekend, Avery barely had time to breathe. Her personal life took a major hit. Regular household chores and personal errands went undone. Maggie's daughter Hanna made her debut in the world. Because of the time already off she would be out eight more weeks instead of twelve. With summer in full swing at the Point Country Club, two months seemed a lifetime away.

What wasn't in the distant future or even right around the corner was Cayden's event. That happened tonight. Avery had been at the club since five that morning, double- and triple-checking her multiple to-do lists to ensure that everything was in place. Now, at three in the afternoon, with the six o'clock cocktail hour fast approaching, she was in her office with shoes off, maxidress hiked to her thighs and head resting against the back of her chair, trying to take a power nap. If only her mind would shut up. If only she'd stop thinking about how it was going to feel to see Cayden. They'd communicated somewhat more frequently as the event drew near but hadn't seen each other since the bingo game and the kiss that wasn't supposed to happen but did. She'd kept each conversation, text and email friendly but professional. Two days ago, she'd invited him over for a final walkthrough of the completed areas but an unexpected trip he had to make to Atlanta changed those plans. Final approval came via video. Neither had brought up the kiss. That hadn't stopped her from thinking about his talented tongue way more than she should, and imagining what it would be like to experience it out of the public eye and all over her body, where they had the whole night to get to know each other.

Avery huffed as her intercom pinged. "Yeah, Charlotte."

"I know, I'm sorry. But the chef wants to know if you can go to the kitchen."

What now?

Produce shortages and delayed shipments had forced last-minute changes to the picnic and brunch menus. She hoped there hadn't been another cancellation. "Did he say why?"

"No. Do you want me to call him back?"

Avery sat up and slipped her feet into her shoes. "That's okay. I need to get going, anyway."

After a quick stop by the loo to freshen up, Avery headed over to the main building, which housed the restaurant and bar, ballroom, pro and gift shop, locker rooms, shower and dressing rooms, and several meeting spaces. July had come in as hot as a firecracker. Avery appreciated the slight breeze she could feel circling beneath her loose-fitting dress. Tonight she'd wear hose, part of the club dress code for management while supervising formal functions, but right now the jersey fabric felt good against bare thighs. She passed the member clubhouse, gym, pool and spa area, and tennis courts. The short walk across the grounds rejuvenated Avery's spirit. She considered herself lucky to work in such a beautiful place.

Avery entered the ballroom and stopped just inside the double doors. She'd already seen it that morning but that made the presentation no less stunning. Crossing through the layout carefully designed for dinner, dancing and social conversation, she reached the hallway leading to the service area and the chef's kitchen where magic happened.

"Lamar, Charlotte said you needed to see me?"

"Yeah." He glanced over his shoulder with a look that didn't include his trademark smile. "Give me a minute to wash my hands."

Avery glanced at the clock on the wall. "I don't have much time."

Lamar dried off and tossed the towel on the counter. "Follow me."

WTH? "Lamar, are you okay? Follow you where?"

Lamar headed out of the kitchen. "There's something in one of the spare rooms that I need to show you."

Before she could argue, Lamar opened a door. "I think you might want to take a look at this."

Then he headed back down the hall.

"Lamar!"

Puzzled and on her way to highly chagrined, Avery stormed over to the opened door. One foot inside and everything changed.

"Cayden! What are you doing here?"

He stood there looking like an afternoon delight, appearing way too seductive in his simple black button-down, casual slacks and loafers.

"I'm getting ready to take your mind off work for a minute and help you relax."

Avery was dumbfounded. "What?"

"Have you eaten today?" He spoke calmly, casually rolling up his shirtsleeves, as though hanging out in storerooms was something he did every day.

Finally tearing her focus away from the vision he presented, Avery's eyes traveled around the modest space. A desk with papers and miscellaneous items strewn about had been pushed against a wall to make way for a serving trolley and a small, round table covered with linen and holding settings for two. She continued her perusal to the other side of the room. *Is that a massage chair?* It was.

No. He. Didn't.

But he had.

Avery was speechless, and incredibly moved. "You did all this?"

"Last night, on the plane ride back to Chicago, I flipped through our communication the past two weeks. Then I thought about the activities that happened during that time, the ones I know about, though there may be more, and came to the conclusion that you've probably been so busy taking care of your clients that you haven't stopped to take care of yourself."

"I'm stunned."

Cayden moved toward the serving trolley next to the table. "And hungry, I hope. Charlotte said she'd brought you a bagel with your coffee but didn't think that you'd had lunch. So I had Lamar whip you up a little something."

"You gave instructions to the chef I hired?" Now, Lamar's terse attitude made sense.

"I asked him to do it and made it worth his while. You'll thank me later, promise."

Avery shook her head. "I can't believe you."

"Yeah, he grumbled a little, too, but I think it was less about making a salad and more about me and not him who would be sharing it with you."

He pulled out a chair. "Sit. Relax. We don't have much time."

Until her first bite of the lightly dressed spinach salad, Avery hadn't realized that she was starved. Topped with tender strips of chateaubriand and served with herbed rolls, the dish was a perfect pick-me-up meal. Substantial, yet light enough to not make her drowsy. Cayden must not have eaten lately, either. There was little conversation as both demolished their plates.

Cayden checked his watch. "Ready for your massage?"

"Really, Cayden. You don't have to do that."

His look could have melted an igloo in subzero temps. "Yes, Avery, I do."

Avery stood up on shaky legs. Inside her head, caution lights flashed and sirens blared. She threw caution to the wind and silenced the bells. Cayden was absolutely right. She needed whatever it was he had in mind.

She straddled the chair and placed her face on the headrest. Cayden adjusted her arms on the pads.

"Relax, and for the next ten minutes try not to think. Okay?"

She nodded.

"Close your eyes."

She did. Nothing happened. Seconds later, the sounds of instrumental neo-soul floated through the room. Then the feel of those fingers she'd dreamed about began kneading her neck and shoulders. The pressure felt so wonderful she could have cried.

"You're so tight," he whispered.

The deep rumble of his whisper made her Kegel muscles tighten more. He placed a thumb at the nape of her neck, pressed and held, before she felt both of his hands massaging upward and into her hair. Thank goodness she'd opted for a simple flat-iron style because she couldn't have brought herself to stop what Cayden was doing. Nor could she silence the moan that slid from her mouth.

"This massage feels amazing."

His hands in her hair was the sweetest arousal, making every inch of her body come alive. Nipples pebbled. Her yoni moistened with dew. The pearl of her paradise throbbed in anticipation. Avery squirmed to squelch the wildfire building. The movement of soft jersey against bare skin inflamed her even more.

Avery lifted her head. "I probably should…but this feels so good."

She held on to the pads and lifted her leg from the side of the chair. Her legs were like jelly. Her body shivered with need. She stumbled back against his chest.

Control fled the room.

Cayden spun her around, their lips colliding in a reunion that was long overdue. She became the aggressor, thrusting her tongue into his hot, wet mouth, her hand running through his soft chestnut curls as he rained kisses down on her face and neck. She felt him harden and thicken against her. She reached down and stroked the length of his dick, wanted to touch it, kiss it, feel it deep inside her.

Cayden pushed an expletive through gritted teeth. In an instant, Avery was off the floor and in his arms.

"What…"

"Shh…" he commanded. "Don't think. Feel."

He laid her on the table, handling her body as though made of porcelain glass. Papers flew one way, markers another. He tugged at the soft jersey material, pulling it over her shins, knees and thighs. Now only a triangle of lace covered her treasure. The feel of cool air from a vent just above them brushed her skin.

Then his tongue took over.

Like a sword, he parted her folds beneath the fabric and dipped his mouth muscle into her fountain of fire. Her mind told her to stop this madness but her body defied her. Legs opened wider. Hips swirled and lifted to give greater access. It was all the encouragement needed. He pulled back the lacy curtain to her main attraction. Avery's fantasy became real when his mouth covered her and he kissed it, long and deep. She tried to scoot away from the painful pleasure but his hands clasped her thighs and held her captive while he nibbled, sucked, kissed and lapped her nectar like a kitty enjoying milk. Her breath increased along with her gyrations. She pulled at her dress and stuffed the scream back into her throat as her body exploded into a million pieces.

Oh. My. God.

She collapsed against the table, working hard to catch her breath. Tender hands pulled at the jersey fabric, smoothing it over her thighs, knees, shins. He pulled her up gently and into his arms. Her essence enveloped them both as they kissed. He slid his hands up her arms, over her shoulders and around her neck.

"There, much better. I think all of the knots are gone. The ballroom looks amazing, by the way. I'm sure everyone will be pleased." He unrolled his sleeves, chatting with the same tongue that had just fucked her senseless, and adjusted his slacks around his slowly deflating erection. "I'll see you in a couple of hours, Ms. Gray."

A wink, and he was out the door. The silence buzzed around her. She dropped into the nearest chair like a sack of potatoes, tried to pull herself together even as she knew one thing for certain, in no uncertain terms. Whatever had just happened, a performance she couldn't begin to describe, could never, ever, *ever* happen between them again.

Thirteen

Cayden rested his back against the cool marble of his walk-in shower and let the rain-forest nozzle pour over him. Palming his sacs in one hand, he ran his other hand along the length of his manhood over and again. Eyes closed he thought of Avery, imagined the taste of her in his mouth. The memory of how eagerly she responded when he placed her on the table made him smile and harden even more. He'd driven over to the country club to make sure Avery ate and to give her a five-minute massage, ten tops. When he spoke with Charlotte over the phone, he learned Avery hadn't eaten lunch. He thought to go online and have something delivered when Charlotte mentioned Lamar. That's when he got the idea that it would be easier and perhaps faster to serve something of what he had prepared or whip something up. Everything happened quickly, spontaneously. He'd enjoyed every minute. Avery hadn't said a word. He didn't know what to think about that, or if once the weekend was over, she'd ever speak to him again.

Finishing his ablutions, he removed his five-o'clock shadow and strode naked and dripping from the master en suite into his customized dressing room and the recently delivered deep blue tuxedo, one of three designer pieces he'd ordered from multimillionaire fashion designer Ace Montgomery's summer collection. His phone buzzed. He picked it up to see that he'd missed several phone calls and more than two dozen texts. Mostly Ma'at members wishing him every success. Almost everyone who'd been invited to the weekend had RSVP'd. He was one step closer to becoming a member of the Society. With that in mind he splashed on his favorite cologne and began to dress.

Less than an hour later, the limo carrying Cayden pulled up to the front entrance of the Point Country Club. Several limos, town cars and luxury sedans lined the horseshoe driveway. A few men, some with their wives, stood on the patio and in the surrounding gardens accepting high-end hors d'oeuvres and flutes of pricey champagne. Everyone appeared to be enjoying themselves. Conversations were animated. Laughter, air kisses and man hugs abounded. Cayden began to relax. He recognized his society mentor, Bob Masters, standing with a distinguished-looking gentleman and a beautiful woman Cayden assumed was the man's wife.

"I'll get out here."

"Are you sure, sir? I can try to maneuver around these cars if you'd like."

"No, this is fine. Did Keri arrange my pickup?"

"Yes, sir. All I need is a text about ten minutes before you're ready to leave. I'll be close by."

"Thanks."

Cayden exited the vehicle and crossed over to the sidewalk. Bob noticed him almost immediately and broke into a smile. He gave Bob a wave and then another to Derrick and Mona, who were standing by the front doors waiting to be checked off the RSVP list and escorted inside. Mona turned and spoke to the woman behind them. Once she turned and smiled, Cayden remembered her face from the Eddington brunch. Delaney Witherspoon. Delaney offered a dainty wave. He nodded. Cayden couldn't deny her beauty. Mona motioned him over. He pointed toward Bob and then to the doors in an unspoken message that told her, *I'll see you inside*. Between now and then he'd try to figure out how to let Mona know that he wasn't interested in her friend's daughter, or anyone else she had in mind. He didn't know what if anything would continue between him and Avery. He wasn't even sure what he wanted to happen. The only thing he knew for sure was that Avery was the only woman on his mind.

He reached Bob and his wife, Hillary, who'd now been joined by another younger couple.

"Greetings, everyone." He gave Bob a fist bump and one-shoulder man hug before bringing Hillary's hand to his lips for a light kiss.

"Cayden, I'd like you to meet some very good friends of mine, members from the west coast. This is Donald Drake of the world-renowned facility Drake Wines Spa and Resort."

"It's a pleasure, sir."

"And his lovely wife, Genevieve."

Cayden held out his hand. "Lovely indeed. Hello, Genevieve."

"As charming as he is handsome," she replied with a wink.

"And this is Donald's brother, Ike, and his beautiful wife, Jennifer. Ike's company boasts some of the best architects in the west. Were they based here, they'd give the Kincaids some serious competition."

Cayden acknowledged the husband and wife. "Thank you all for coming."

"We never like to miss a chance to do good."

"What she means is she never likes to miss a chance to shop on Lake Shore Drive."

Everyone laughed, a perfect time for Cayden to excuse himself. He greeted a few more people before entering the club lobby. It was comfortably filled with America's elite. Men in tuxedos or suits. Women gowned in silk and satin. Hair and makeup done to perfection. Colorful clutches and bling everywhere. Cayden guessed that were a robbery to occur, the jewelry in this room alone would make the assailant an instant billionaire. The light sound of traditional jazz flowed through the speakers and mingled with the clink of crystal and the murmur of cultured voices. After working the lobby to greet those not deeply engaged in conversation, he walked toward the ballroom. He was just about to enter when someone called his name.

He turned around and smiled at the well-dressed couple walking toward him. "Bruce. My man!"

Cayden was excited to see that one of his buddies from Northwestern had made it. His smile almost faltered when he saw the woman walking beside him. Her new asymmetrical hairstyle with feathery bangs gave

Teagan a totally different appearance. He almost didn't recognize her.

"How are you, brother?" Bruce said.

"Everything's good, man." They performed an intricate handshake. "Glad you could make it."

"Do you know Teagan? She attended Northwestern the same time as us."

"We took a couple classes together." Cayden nodded toward her. "Teagan."

"Hello, again. I was surprised when Bruce mentioned this glorious affair. When we saw each other at First Friday, you never said a thing."

There was a reason.

He turned his attention to Bruce. "I've other guests to greet. You two enjoy yourselves."

Nearing the ballroom, memories of what had happened with Avery a short few hours ago flipped through his mind. He shut down the mental images and reached for one of the double doors. Just as he began to walk through them, someone came out. Too bad her head was turned in the opposite direction.

"Whoa, there."

"Ooh, excu— Cayden."

Avery quickly averted her eyes but Cayden couldn't drink in enough of her. The color of her simple, one-shoulder gown boasting an oversize bow cinching an hourglass figure was an almost exact match to his tuxedo. A closer examination revealed tiny ruby-colored pinstripes, further emphasized by the same color of red-bottomed stilettos. Sparkly pins secured loosely curled hair piled on top of her head, with a few errant tendrils brushing her neck the way his lips longed to do. Her makeup was minimal but effective, especially the glossy lipstick that reminded him of how she'd swirled her tongue with his in an oral dance as old as time. There was only word for how Avery looked. Perfect. He'd like to think he had something to do with that glow to her skin.

"We've got to stop meeting like this."

"I'm sorry. Charlotte called out to me just as the door opened."

He wanted to tell her that she could slam her body into his whenever she liked but her professional demeanor told him that now was not the time.

"Is everything okay?"

Finally, her eyes met his. "Yes."

"No last-minute snafus to worry about?"

"There was an earlier issue with the extra pounds of Breedlove beef we ordered but we got it resolved."

"Good. I see you got the midnight blue memo."

Avery ran a hand down her dress. "I didn't realize it, but yes, the message must have come through."

"You look amazing."

Her eyes shifted away from him again, discomfort as bright as the sparkly pins she wore. "Thank you. The program will begin promptly at seven. The maître d' will make an announcement now for the guests to move inside."

She continued past him without a goodbye, see you later or kiss my boots. Definitely not the actions of a satiated woman delighted to run into her lover. He shook off the disappointment and entered the ballroom. There were too many other things to worry about than Avery's feelings right now. Still, he made a mental note not to leave before they'd had a conversation. Much as she'd felt about the kiss creating an awkward working relationship, her not wanting to talk to him about the storeroom would create an even greater tension that neither needed.

The evening ran smoothly. Cayden felt he blinked and three hours went by. Raelynn Parker, a popular newscaster and Point du Sable native, emceed the evening and kept the night lively. Short speeches were delivered by himself, Bob Masters, SOMA's president and a couple celebrity members. The Roulette sisters, founders of THAT Pink, were honored as the evening's special guests. Aside from Mona's displeasure when Cayden hid behind hosting duties to avoid sitting next to Delaney during dinner, everyone seemed pleased with what he'd put together. The weekend wasn't over yet. One day down, two to go.

Cayden didn't see Avery again until after the dinner service when the swinging jazz sounds of the live band coaxed guests to the dance floor. He was standing in the lobby speaking with one of his college buddies when he saw her head outside. Quickly excusing himself from the conversation, he hurried to catch up with her.

"Avery!"

He saw her back stiffen before she turned around.

"Can we talk?"

"I'm still working."

"This won't take long."

She didn't reply but didn't run off, either. Cayden walked them a distance away from the entrance. This was a conversation for their ears alone.

"If I said I was sorry about what happened earlier today, again, I'd be lying. But I do apologize if what took place has made this weekend harder or stressed you out in any way."

She crossed her arms, looking down at the ground. "I guess you got what you came for."

"I came to make sure you'd eaten and give you a brief massage. Everything else just happened."

"Is that what you've told yourself?" Avery's eyes flashed fire.

"Are you blaming me for what occurred? Maybe I should have pumped the brakes, but you were far from being an unwilling participant."

"You knew I was vulnerable."

"I *believed* you were tired, overworked and could use a little TLC."

"And ripe to be taken advantage of."

That was a low blow. Cayden took a step back. It took restraint, but he kept his voice low and calm. "You don't believe that."

"Don't I? You and your cozy, romantic dinner setup, linen, soft music, a table for two—"

"In a storage room. Don't leave out that part."

"And offering a massage. Have you ever had a client do that?"

"A chair, for a head, neck and shoulder massage."

"When you knew full well that you had something else in mind."

"Seriously? If my plan all along was just to fuck you, I would have replaced the chair with a table and told you to get buck naked as soon as you walked into the room."

"Oh, no, you're much too suave for that. Instead, you used manipulation. If someone found out, I could lose my job!"

"Fine! If that's what you want to believe, go for it. I know what I intended. The scenario you've painted is not what happened and the person you've described is not who I am!"

A nanosecond from saying something he couldn't take

back, Cayden spun around and headed back toward the building.

"Cayden!"

He kept walking. Whatever Avery wanted to say didn't matter. Perhaps she had a right to be angry, but thinking he'd take advantage of any woman had made him mad as hell.

Fourteen

Avery made a beeline for the club's executive offices and dared herself to cry. Five-inch red bottoms made her feet look sexy but trying to bust a fast move on concrete made them hurt like hell. She clenched her hands into fists and kept on walking, asking herself what just happened for the second time that day. And why had he invited that woman from First Friday, the one who'd accosted her in the bathroom? The one he said he barely knew.

She quickly pulled out her key to open the door. Once inside, she leaned her body against it, closed her eyes and worked to regulate her breathing. She slid out of her shoes and if she'd had her way the dress and body-shaping undergarment would have followed right behind them. That wasn't possible. She had a job to do. That thought in mind, she pushed away from the door and headed into her office. She crossed to her desk, sat down and retrieved her tablet from the drawer. Her finger hovered over the power button. The words from her argument with Cayden rang fresh in her ears. What she said wasn't truly how she felt so why had she attacked him? Why had she played the victim card and blamed him for what happened?

Because you don't want to face your real feelings and admit that you care about him.

Avery stood and paced from her desk to the window. Earlier when they'd collided, her knees had gone weak. It should have been unlawful for a man to be that handsome, for a body to be able to bless a suit like that. She'd felt instant desire and ran away. That was the truth plain and simple. Her plan was to try to avoid him for the rest of the night.

How'd that work out for you?

It hadn't, and that was the problem. When he called out to her she couldn't ignore him, not with his friends looking on and other guests, too. She knew they needed to talk, but she wasn't ready. When he admitted he enjoyed what had happened as much as she had, it scared her. If he gave chase, she doubted her willpower would be strong enough to push him away. Avery had determined keeping him at arm's length was exactly what she needed to do. For many reasons. Starting with the fact that he'd committed a crime and from the looks of things had gotten away with it. Brittany had tricked her into delivering the envelope to First Bank, the packet that contained the information of Cayden's embezzlement, but when she learned what he'd planned to do, she was glad that she'd helped stop it. The Cayden of today seemed to be nothing like the one Brittany had told her about, but how much could a person really change?

Then there was the fact that she'd broken a company rule. And on the property, no less! When it came to finances, Avery lived rather conservatively. She had a modest portfolio. If she got fired or lost her job, she wouldn't starve. But she'd worked hard to get where she was and had beat out dozens of applicants to be the club's assistant event director. Cayden's charity event was her chance to prove she'd been the right one to hire. Sleeping with the client would convey it had been a really bad idea.

Finally, there was her love life's track record. Not very good. The last relationship with the very married single guy left her heartbroken and distrustful. Her clue that it wasn't his first rodeo in adultery was how good he was at covering it up. Her ex was a consummate liar, always able to explain away his long absences when he'd leave to be with the family that was ensconced in another state.

No, right now Avery didn't need to think about jumping into a relationship with Cayden or anyone else. But since he was still her client and they would be in each other's presence for two more days, she did need to seek him out, offer him an apology and let him off the hook for what happened today. Cayden was right. It took two to tango. She'd thoroughly enjoyed the dance.

After retrieving the contact information needed regarding tomorrow's kickoff, she went looking for him. She'd acknowledged to herself that it was her attraction to Cayden that made her lash out, and the part she'd played in what happened. Now it was time to be honest with him.

Gathering the info she'd come for, she pulled out the makeup bag she stashed for emergencies and quickly powdered off the shine from the July humidity and swiped on a coat of lip gloss. She slipped into the stilettos, did a quick check around the office, then closed and locked the door behind her. Daylight had given way to dusk, bringing with it a slightly cooler breeze. The tendrils Touché had left hanging down brushed against her neck. Once again she was reminded of what happened earlier, the feel of Cayden's lips as he branded her skin. She'd walked—or wobbled was probably a more accurate description—out of that storeroom feeling infinitely more relaxed than when she went in, which made her feel even more guilty about how she lashed out at him. Yep, she needed to fix that. The sooner, the better.

She decided to take a shortcut by cutting across the tennis court area and entering the main building through a side door. Out of the plentiful lighting that covered the front patio and surrounding areas Avery got an eerie feeling, as though she was being followed, or watched. She stopped and looked around her. The only sounds heard were those of the cicadas, the only shadows made by tree branches dancing to their song. She shook off the uncomfortable sensation and continued toward the ballroom. When she reached the hallway leading to the lobby, she slowed her pace, took a breath and slipped on her professional HWIC face. At the moment she didn't feel like the head woman in charge, but if looking the part was half the battle, she was on her way to winning when she reached the lobby floor.

Seeing that Cayden wasn't among those mingling in that area, she stepped into the ballroom. Contemporary dance music had replaced the live jazz band taking a break. The music was bumping, the floor crowded. She moved from one side of the room to the other, looking for a tuxedo the color of midnight blue, and caught a glimpse of it on the dance floor. Pushing aside the thought to wait until the song ended, Avery waded into the sea of dancing bodies and bobbing heads. In her mind this was an emergency that couldn't wait. Or so she thought, until catching a full view of Cayden and, even more, his dancing partner, an incredibly beautiful woman one couldn't help but notice. Avery had done so earlier during the dinner service. She'd been seated next to Mona Eddington and a man Avery had assumed was her date. If the way the stunner looked at Cayden was any indication, Avery had been wrong on that count. What if she were Cayden's date, and he'd been off socializing when Avery had passed by? He was already upset with her. Would it make him even angrier to interrupt his dance?

Avery didn't know but she was about to find out.

She maneuvered around the last few dancers separating her from the goal, then tapped Cayden on the shoulder.

"I'm sorry to interrupt but we have an emergency."

Cayden looked from her to Delaney. "What's going on?"

"Sorry," Avery said to Delaney, who pointedly ignored her. And then back to Cayden. "Can you come with me? This shouldn't take long."

Cayden looked dubious. He eyed Avery for a second longer before speaking to Delaney. "I apologize. Allow me to escort you back to the table."

"It's okay." Delaney placed a possessive hand on Cayden's arm. "Handle your business, darling. When you return, I'll be ready for the next dance."

With a wink and a smile that would sell beef to vegans, she walked off. Avery tried not to acknowledge the feelings that arose as she watched a woman with the perfect everything glide into the crowd. But as she and Cayden entered the lobby and then a meeting room just beyond it, the perception that she was being less than smart would not go away. They may not be in high school anymore, but she'd most likely still become invisible to Cayden whenever women like Ms. Perfect came around. So what did it matter if he were angry, or whatever way he felt about her? There was no future with a man like him. Two more days and their forced connection would be over. Belatedly, Avery realized she should have left well-enough alone.

"What is the emergency, Avery? What is so important that I had to be interrupted?"

The door had barely closed behind them before Cayden reacted, making Avery even more sure that this was a mistake. He was probably anxious to get back to his date. Best to get this over and done with.

"The question of whether or not this weekend is a failure or success."

This got his attention. He leaned against the wall and crossed his arms. "I'm listening."

"We might disagree on many things, but what both of us want is for this event to be successful. That can go more smoothly if we're getting along." Avery ignored his snort and continued.

"We've both been under a lot of pressure. Speaking for myself, anxiety has been high. Not only am I fairly new to this job but I had to grab the reins and ride solo much faster than expected. I know my job situation has nothing to do with you, but I wanted to provide some perspective. Getting hired here was not easy. Dozens vied for the position. When Maggie went on leave, I was secretly terrified. It became even more important that I rise to the challenge and make sure that all of the club's clients received the type of service that the Point is known for, the stellar outcomes this community has come to expect."

Cayden shifted, as if to speak.

"Just hear me out." Avery lifted a halting hand. "Please."

Cayden said nothing, but Avery noted his body relaxed the tiniest bit.

"From the time I ran into you, literally, I've been in a battle with myself. Fighting off a crazy attraction I thought had been left behind in our high school years. I told myself that whatever I felt wasn't a big deal. We travel in different circles, and even though I felt that in working at the city's most popular high-society hangout we'd more than likely run into each other, I figured it would be in passing. When I came into the lobby that day to greet my first client, I thought my eyes were playing tricks on me. I couldn't believe it was you."

Cayden looked at his watch. Avery cut to the chase.

"What happened in the storage room earlier today wasn't your fault. I don't believe it was something you planned. It just happened, and I was glad that it did. I wanted it, enjoyed it, as much as you did. Probably more. Our making love…"

Cayden arched a brow.

"Okay, making out…was actually just what I needed. Those knots you felt were from built-up stress. Worry had me feeling as tight as a drum. Instead of lashing out at you, I should have said thanks. Not only because of your thoughtful gesture, wanting to know that I was okay, but for being a gracious and easygoing client. After doing weddings and other personal celebrations at Lake Chalet, believe me, you've made planning this event a joy. All of that to say I'm sorry for my earlier accusations. I didn't feel manipulated and know what happened wasn't planned. I wanted to clear the air now, tonight, and remove any animosity or bad feeling between us. I've heard nothing but praise from the guests so far and wanted to do my part to make sure that continues."

Avery felt spent, and emotionally naked. Being transparent with her feelings wasn't easy. Cayden's eyes were dark, and unreadable. He remained silent. She couldn't do anything about that. The only person she could control was herself. From then on out Avery was going to put what happened behind her and be the consummate professional.

"Well, that's all I wanted to say. I'm sure you're ready to get back to your guests. Thanks for listening."

"You're welcome."

Avery watched as Cayden silently left the room, leaving her to wonder if being honest had made an impact. Her not having time to dwell on it was probably a good thing. The dance was winding down. Many guests had left already. Soon it would be time to gather the remaining staff and get ready for tomorrow. With that in mind, Avery left the meeting room on her way to housekeeping. As she entered the lobby, a commotion near the clubhouse drew her attention. Two security guards and the hostess who'd handled the VIP list were speaking with someone out of vision, a person animatedly using their hands.

The younger of the two guards saw Avery approach and left the doorway to meet her. They stopped a few feet away.

"What's going on, Ralph?"

"Some woman demanding that she be admitted, even though her name isn't on the list."

Avery was thankful it wasn't something more serious. "I'll take care of it."

The two of them continued to the door, hearing the woman's voice raise along with her agitation.

"I'm telling you, I was invited! Get me the manager, now!"

Avery reached the door. The guard stepped back so she could speak to the guest.

"Excuse me, I'm the manager here. May I help you?"

The woman, who'd been busy texting on her phone, jerked her head up when Avery spoke. Several seconds passed before recognition dawned.

"Brittany?"

Brittany's eyes narrowed. "Avery? You're… Oh, never mind. Thank God it's you. I tried to tell these men I belonged here."

She made a move toward the door. The guard blocked her.

"I'm sorry, Brittany," Avery said, working to keep a pleasant tone to her voice. "But this is a private event."

The hostess held out her tablet. "I've searched the list twice, Avery. Her name isn't there."

Avery made a show of checking a list she knew by heart. After several seconds, she looked up. "I'm sorry, Brittany, but the people hosting this event were very clear that only invited guests could attend."

"By people you mean Cayden Barker, correct?"

Avery didn't try to hide her surprise. "You know it's his event and you're trying to crash it?"

"I have my reasons."

"Perhaps, but I can't go against the rules."

"I thought we were friends," Brittany said with a pout.

"I did, too." Avery took several steps away from the

entrance to make their talk more private. "But that was before you left town without a goodbye to me or Lisa."

"I regret that, Avery." Brittany stood close to Avery, her voice now lowered and calm. "Can we talk about it? Later, maybe, when you have time."

"Sure." Avery pulled out her phone. "What's your number?"

Brittany reeled it off, her eyes glued to the entrance doors. "Can you at least tell Cayden I'm out here? I really need to speak with him, too."

"There you are," Charlotte said, rushing toward the two women talking. "One of the PDS board members needs to see you, ASAP."

"I have to go," Avery said to Brittany. "I'll call you."

Avery could have kissed Charlotte for her timing. The interruption prevented her from having to lie to a former friend. The last thing she wanted to do was tell Cayden about Brittany. She meant what she'd said about calling her, though. She had questions. Brittany had answers. The two definitely needed to talk.

Avery thought work would slow down once the tournament was over, but it felt like the opposite had occurred. Maggie returned to work that following Monday, a couple weeks earlier than scheduled, demanding reports that Avery hadn't yet prepared and a detailed spreadsheet of upcoming events. Cayden had called but she hadn't returned it. She hadn't called Brittany, either. Today was Wednesday, the first time all week she'd left the office before the sun went down. On her way to the car, she pulled out her phone to call him. More than likely he had a question regarding the past weekend, a conversation that wouldn't take long.

"This is Cayden."

The sound of his voice brought goose bumps. She willed her body to behave. "Cayden, it's Avery."

"Hi."

"Hi." He sounded nervous, too. Not angry. Good. "Sorry it took so long to get back with you."

"It's okay. I hope you enjoyed your time off."

"I will when I take it. Maggie returned to work this week. It's been super busy getting her caught up. Look, if this is about what happened…"

"It is and it isn't."

"What does that mean?"

"I do think we have a lot to talk about, but mainly the call was about the effort you put into ensuring the golf tournament's success."

"I was only doing my job."

"How would you like to take a break from said job and get away for the weekend?"

Avery had no idea where that segue was headed. "I'd be happy to take a break and do nothing."

"Great idea, especially if that doing nothing was in California."

Avery wasn't sure she'd heard him correctly. "California?"

"Yeah, you know that big state on the west coast just above Mexico?"

"So you got an A in geography. Goody for you."

Cayden's unabashed laughter brought a smile to her face. She'd missed talking to this man.

"One of my guests from the fundraiser owns a resort. He invited me out for a visit this weekend. Would you like to come?"

Like I did when you sent me over the moon in the store-room? Hell, yeah! But he probably meant on the trip.

"Wow, Cayden, that's some kind of invitation. California sounds wonderful but…"

"I know. We've had our moments. Flared tempers. Misunderstandings. All while trying to juggle a multi-million-dollar fundraiser. It was a lot. We were both stressed. I figured a weekend getaway would give us a chance to have a real conversation and clear everything up. I went online to check it out. The place looks fantastic. There's no ulterior motive. I'd book separate rooms. With all of the events that take place at the club, we'll more than likely be seeing each other. It would be great to develop a friendship, if only for business reasons. I would say take some time and get back with me but—"

"I don't need time to think about it. I'd love to come with you."

"Excellent. I'll text over the information. We can talk again after that."

"I appreciate this, Cayden. Thank you."

"You're welcome."

Same two words as the other night. Totally different delivery. Rather than dissect what the invitation meant she chose to be thankful that he'd asked her. She received Cayden's text, then placed a call to Maggie and got the time off. She almost called Brittany, then decided against it. Avery deserved a vacation and wanted to spend time with Cayden. Why her old friend was back in town and crashing club parties could wait until she returned from California.

Fifteen

Cayden considered himself a sophisticated, successful man. But today he felt like that ten-year-old who thought Jake's house was a hotel. For his trip to California, Derrick had generously given Cayden the use of his private plane. Flying in the sleek, fully customized Gulfstream 550 wasn't new. He'd crisscrossed the country on business trips and gone on vacation with Jake and sometimes the other Eddington siblings at least a dozen times. But he'd never been offered solo use of the plane for business or pleasure and couldn't wait to see Avery's reaction upon learning that they were traveling to wine country in style.

He didn't have to wait. The car service he'd sent to pick her up arrived on schedule. He instructed the driver to handle the luggage and opened the back door. Avery took the hand he offered and got out of the car.

"Good morning!"

"Obviously a very good morning," she replied, her eyes scanning the airstrip before coming to rest on the plane. "I thought getting picked up in a limo was fancy. What is going on?"

"We're flying to California."

"We're flying private?" Cayden nodded as they walked to the airstairs. "However you pulled this off, I'm impressed."

"I didn't have to go far and didn't ask for the favor. This flight comes courtesy of Derrick Eddington."

"You must make that company a lot of money. That's a very generous gift."

"Probably more like a pacifier for frustrating delays happening on the job. But I don't want to talk about that. In fact, how about we make topics of work off-limits for the weekend."

"Works for me."

The pilot and flight attendant stood just inside the door. After introductions came the tour. Avery's awe at the extravagance inside Derrick's fly baby boasting the company colors caused Cayden to see them with new eyes. The plane was designed for multiple configurations, comfortably holding up to eighteen passengers and four crew. Because it would only be Cayden and Avery on the flight, he'd requested the L3 configuration that in addition to the calfskin-covered swivel seats up front included a living area with full-size sofa, dining section with minibar, full-size bathroom and sleeping quarters.

"I could easily live here," Avery said as they sat and buckled up to prepare for takeoff.

"It would be the most expensive studio apartment ever rented."

The flight attendant came over with mimosas. "This looks like a celebration so here you go, guys!"

"It is indeed." Cayden held up his glass.

So did Avery. "To what are we toasting?"

"To a stellar and successful fundraiser, the woman largely responsible for making it happen and a relaxing, stress-free time in California."

"Thank you, Cayden. You worked hard, also, so cheers to you."

They clinked glasses and continued chatting casually as the plane reached cruising altitude and the flight attendant began the meal service.

Avery finished a bite of salad. "Will this be your first time in Napa Valley?"

"That's not where we're headed."

"Oh, my bad. I thought you mentioned wine country."

"Southern California's wine country. We're going to Temecula."

"Never heard of it."

"I've passed it when driving from Los Angeles to San Diego. But I've never been to the resort, which is supposed to be amazing. The wines produced there have received numerous awards."

The dinner plates had been taken and dessert was on the way before Cayden broached the topic on both of their minds.

"We need to talk about what happened in the storeroom."

"Okay." Avery picked up her glass of sparkling water and took a sip.

"Are you still angry about it?"

"I was never angry, to tell you the truth. I was stunned, confused, really turned on...but never angry. What you heard when I went off on you that night was fear. A rule at the club says that we can't date or go out with clients. On a more personal note, I definitely feel an attraction. That scares me, too."

"Why?"

"Because there's nowhere for that feeling to go. Point du Sable is too small for casual hookups, and even if it weren't, I'm not that girl."

"I'm not that guy, either. Definitely not a fan of the gossip mill. But who says this has to be casual? You're attracted to me. I'm feeling you, too. Perhaps we should go with those feelings and see what happens."

"Just because something sounds wonderful doesn't mean it's wise."

Cayden grinned. "That sounds like something Miss Kay would say."

"Hey, where was she this past weekend? I'm surprised you didn't invite her to the ball."

"I did. She'd already made plans to visit her sister in Michigan."

"That's where she's from?" Cayden nodded. "Detroit?"

"Kalamazoo."

"I was surprised to see your friend from Northwestern at the gala."

"No more than I was."

"You didn't invite her?"

Cayden shook his head. "Her date, Bruce, also went there. He's a good friend of mine. As I said before, I hardly know Teagan. She would never have received an invite from me."

Someone else had stopped by the club that night, someone he'd never wanted to see again, let alone invite anywhere. Cayden hadn't been happy to learn that Brittany was in town and wanted to talk, even though he'd agreed with Jake that perhaps she'd grown a conscience and wanted to apologize for the hell her lies had put him through. Did Avery know her friend was back in the Point? Probably so, but she didn't mention it and Cayden didn't ask. The last person he wanted to talk about during this vacation was Brittany Moore.

The conversation shifted. He pulled up the website for Drake Wines Resort and Spa. Checking out their amenities, activities and attractions got both of them excited. By the time the plane began its descent into French Valley Airport, they'd mapped out a rough itinerary covering all three days. Avery seemed lighter, freer, than she did when they'd boarded the plane in Point du Sable. It felt good to see her relaxed and carefree. Her enthusiasm was contagious. It took his mind off Brittany and the unfortunate timing of her visit. He decided not to worry about it. As long as there was no contact and she kept his name out of her mouth, he'd successfully complete his SOMA probation and everyone would get along fine.

Sixteen

Avery wasn't unaccustomed to luxury. She'd stayed in her fair share of five-star hotels. But from the moment the limo turned onto the tree-lined road leading up to Drake Wines Resort and Spa, she knew this was about to be a different experience with a type of opulence she'd never seen. A deft landscaper had managed to make one feel as though they'd entered a personal paradise far away from the hubbub. In fact, they were within the city limits of Temecula, a town that according to the Drake Wines website was home to over a hundred thousand residents. The rolling hills and tall, mature trees behind a white picket fence that gleamed in the sun was as calming as it was picturesque. She relaxed into the soft, rich leather, allowing the tenseness created when they'd discussed "the incident" and Teagan to fully dissipate. There was a lot to unpack from that conversation. She'd do so later, when alone in her room. Now, she wanted to stay present and enjoy every inch of this wonderful place.

"Thanks again, Cayden, for inviting me on this trip. I can't get over the beauty here."

"You haven't seen anything yet," the driver informed her. "Sorry to eavesdrop, but it's the truth."

The driver was right. They pulled up to a structure as grand as any she'd seen. Fountains and artfully cut shrubbery lined the cobblestone round the limo pulled into, along with a statue of a man working in a vineyard. A smartly dressed attendant opened her door and extended his hand.

"Welcome to Drake Wines Resort and Spa," he sang in a Caribbean-tinged accent.

Avery exited the car. "Thank you. I love it already."

Immediately after a wave of heat rolled over her body she felt the cooling breeze of an air-conditioning vent from some unseen but heavenly source. In Chicago's hot summer months the humidity could be unyielding. She made a mental note to inquire about whatever system they used and see if the same were feasible for the Point's outdoor living spaces.

"May I have the name on the reservation, please?"

Cayden joined them on the car's passenger side. "Barker. Cayden Barker."

"Thank you, sir." The attendant motioned to a porter standing just inside the rotating doors. He grabbed a luggage cart and walked to the opened trunk.

"If you will proceed to the reservation desk directly ahead, one of our front desk personnel will take it from here. Enjoy your stay at Drake Wines Resort and Spa."

The receptionist smiled warmly as she greeted them. "Mr. Drake sends his regrets at not being able to personally greet you, but has extended a dinner invitation for tomorrow evening, if you're free. A card bearing the details has been placed in your suite, along with other welcome amenities. You've also been assigned a personal butler who will work to ensure your every comfort. His name is Gustav. He will ring you shortly, then come up for a proper introduction."

Avery's head was spinning before seeing the room. Personal greetings from the hotel owner, and a butler to boot? She was living in rarified air. As they crossed over to the elevators, a thought hit her.

"Did they give you two key cards?"

Cayden pulled a second gold card from the pouch and handed it to her.

"You only booked one room?"

"Yes, but don't worry. It's a two-bedroom suite. If after seeing it you still would prefer completely separate accommodations, I'll have Gustav take care of it right away."

The luxury suites were all named after wines. Cayden stopped outside "Burgundy." Once inside the cavernous space, Avery thought of her concern of one room, one bed and laughed out loud. The suite was almost the size of her two-bedroom condo with two matching master suites separated by a living room large enough to comfortably hold a grand piano, a full-size kitchen and formal dining room. On the dining room table was a welcoming basket wrapped in transparent gold foil and tied with a burgundy bow. Avery released her luggage handle and walked into the dining room.

"This is lovely," she said over her shoulder to Cayden. "Want to see what's in it?"

He walked up next to her and reached for the card pinned to the bow. "It's from Donald."

"Donald Drake, a guest at your party."

"One and the same. He says, 'Dear Cayden and Avery, Welcome to Drake Wines Resort and Spa. Please accept my apologies for not being able to personally greet you by joining my wife, Genevieve, and me for dinner tomorrow evening, followed by a special concert you won't want to miss.'"

He tossed the card on the table. "Want to go?"

"Sure, why not?"

Avery continued pulling items from the basket. Cayden looked on. Gourmet chocolates, smoked salmon and caviar with toast points, a variety of cheeses and bottles of alkaline water were perfect complements to a bottle of the vineyard's finest champagne and two crystal flutes. Thoughtfully designed with the traveler in mind, the silk-covered rectangular design of the collapsible basket allowed it to be easily packed away as a memento.

Cayden picked up the bottle of champagne. "This looks like good stuff. Should we pop the cork?"

He wriggled his brows in a way meant to be funny but had Avery's insides feeling butterflies.

"It needs to chill." *So do I.* "Doesn't the tour for first-time guests start soon?"

"In about an hour, I think."

"Then I'm going to get unpacked and freshen up. Meet you back here in, say, forty-five?"

In a totally unexpected move, Cayden pulled her into his arms for a hug that for Avery was both too long and not nearly long enough, and kissed her cheek. "Thank you for agreeing to come with me. I'm glad you're here."

"Me, too."

Avery eased out of the hug and made a beeline for her luggage and master suite. Her thoughts—not to mention hormones—were all over the place. She needed to get a grip. As soon as she'd closed the door, she pulled out her phone and called Lisa.

"I was just thinking about you," was Lisa's greeting. "How's it going?"

"Like a dream that I don't want to wake from. What about you?"

"Just endured a nightmare. I saw Brittany."

"Really? Where?"

"The Upscale boutique. She was all hugs and smiles and gushing over Amanda, as though she hadn't dropped me like a sack of rotten potatoes ten-plus years ago."

"Dang. Bitter much?"

"Who, *moi*?" The sisters laughed. "I don't hate her. I just see through the fakeness and don't want any part of it. I guess you don't, either, since she said you still haven't called."

"I know. I need to."

"Does Cayden know she's back?"

"I don't think so. He didn't mention her."

"But he knows the two of you used to be friends."

"Yeah, we talked about that." It's what they hadn't discussed that now worried Avery. Even with the questions she still had for Brittany, Avery no longer felt so good about the part she'd played in Cayden's scandal. "Look, sis, I need to run. Just wanted to let you know that we arrived safely."

"Have fun, okay?"

Avery took a deep breath. "I'll try."

"Shouldn't be hard. He's a good-looking man."

"That he is. I love you, Lisa."

"Love you, too."

Avery walked into the living room determined to forget about the goings-on in Chicago and enjoy this paradise. Cayden made that easy. He stood on the balcony looking exceptional in a short-sleeved baby blue button-down and a pair of white shorts that showed off his tan. She didn't even try to stop the flutters. He must have felt her eyes on him because he suddenly turned around and came into the room. As he took in her floral baby-doll mini and comfy sandals, a smile slowly lit up his face. The perusal was sensuous. Almost as sexy as him.

"Ready?" she asked.

"Yes. For anything."

They met the tour guide in the lobby and for the next hour, along with several other couples, were shown what made Drake Wines Resort and Spa an award-winning location. Aside from learning everything about wine-making, guests could swim, play tennis or miniature golf, hike, ride horseback, fish and take advantage of any number of indoor activities. Everyone was friendly but Avery noticed how they all gravitated to Cayden, who was entirely adorable just being himself. During the tour, a camaraderie developed between them and a married couple who lived in South Carolina. The husband, Owen, was an investment banker. His wife, Violet, designed jewelry that she sold on the internet. They were funny and down-to-earth. By the end of the tour they felt like old friends. So much so that when Owen suggested they check out the nearby casino the tour guide had mentioned, Avery and Cayden agreed.

What a great idea! Neither Avery nor Cayden were big gamblers. They had much more fun watching Owen at the blackjack table and Violet yell at the slots. After a few rounds of win-lose-win, the couples ate dinner at the casino and then headed toward the sound of a live band playing remixes from the early 2000s. Cayden pulled Avery on the dance floor.

Pumping his hips to the beat, Cayden inched closer to her. "Do you remember what happened the last time we danced?"

"How could I forget?" That kiss and the afternoon in the storeroom was often the mental images that accompanied her to sleep.

He laughed and ran a finger down her cheek. His eyes smoldered. She knew what was on his mind. It was on hers, too. Still, Avery didn't want to rush into bed with Cayden. Something told her that once she experienced the full extent of his pleasure, he would be a hard habit to break. Owen and Violet shimmied and shook their way next to them, breaking the spell Cayden was weaving around her. Violet danced like a video vixen. Owen was a goof. Great fun, but after several songs Avery began feeling the effects of the early rising.

"I'm going to text the service," she told Cayden, referring to the complimentary car the resort provided. "It's time for me to call it a night."

"I'm ready, too."

They left their newfound friends grooving on the dance floor and in no time at all were back within the confines of their beautiful suite. Avery wasn't a chicken, but she knew she needed distance from Cayden right now.

"Tonight was awesome." She stretched and yawned. "I feel jet-lagged, though, and believe I'll head toward a good night's sleep."

Cayden walked over and reached for her hands. "Are you sure? I was thinking about going down to that game room, maybe play a round of pool. See how well you handle a stick."

By the tone of his voice and the look in his eyes, Avery knew exactly what he meant.

She couldn't help but flirt back. "After a good night's sleep, I'll be ready for anything."

He slid an arm around her waist and pulled her to him. "Promise?"

"Don't want to make one I might not keep."

"I can respect that. All right, then, angel—" he kissed her forehead "—sweet dreams." He slid his mouth to hers and covered it. The exchange quickly deepened as tongues touched and swayed. This time it was Cayden who pulled back.

"I'd better stop before this gets out of hand. Not because I don't want you, Avery. But because of how much I do."

"Good night, Cayden."

Avery went to her room, quickly undressed and was soon hugging a soft body pillow instead of the tempting hard body just a few yards away. Today, she'd been able to withstand that temptation. Tomorrow...all bets were off.

Seventeen

Cayden's dick was hard enough to cut granite. It took everything in him to end the kiss and walk away. Through his discomfort, he made it across floors covered in mosaic marble and boasting silk Esfahān rugs Cayden imagined were priced in the millions, and over to the fully stocked built-in bar. He pulled down a snifter with one hand and a bottle of ultra-aged, single-malt Scotch with the other, poured himself a finger full and threw it back. Velvety smoothness gave way to a slow burn that accompanied the amber-colored liquor on its journey from throat to stomach. It settled there, casting off warmth like a wood-burning furnace. His raging member calmed. With his third leg subdued, he could walk without discomfort. He poured himself another finger of Scotch and continued through the airy, richly appointed room to the attached balcony. It was a beautiful night. The stars were plentiful and the moon almost full. A patio set with an umbrella occupied one side of the space. A chaise on the other. Cayden sat on one of the patio seats and wondered how in the heck he ever thought sharing a suite with Avery, even one with a huge living space between bedrooms, was a good idea. A slew of beautiful women had graced Cayden's bed, but he couldn't remember ever desiring a woman the way he did Avery in this moment. Slouching down he rested his head on the back of the chair, looked at the stars and sipped his drink. He was in paradise with the best of everything, including a beautiful woman. One who wanted friendship, no benefits. It was going to be a long night.

Cayden awakened to the soft sound of a chime. He opened one eye and mentally clawed past the fog in his brain. What the hell happened last night? Shifting, he saw a snifter on the nightstand. *Whiskey. Right.* The fine and rare Macallan 1926, best in the world, was how Donald's note had described it. Cayden had always been a lightweight. He yawned and struggled to a sitting position. There it was again, the soft tinkling of chimes.

Avery?

A bell sounded, engaging the front door speaker. "Mr. Barker, it's Gustav, sir. I've come to help you get dressed for your first appointment."

What time was it? "Where's Aver… Ms. Gray?" Cayden lumbered out of bed and stretched. The sun had risen in the eastern sky, blanketing lush green hills rolling into row upon row of grapevines that seemed to go on forever. A bright red barn stood to the left of the grapevines. Cattle and horses grazed both inside and outside of tall white picket fences surrounding several buildings.

"Ms. Gray has already showered and gone downstairs.

She'll meet you at Enlighten for your scheduled morning meditation and dance class. Sir, there is a button on the nightstand to open the door."

Cayden pushed the button. He pulled on a baggy pair of gray-flannel drawstring pants and padded barefoot toward the smell of coffee. Gustav met him in the hall. "Breakfast will be ready upon your return."

Exactly twenty-two minutes later, Cayden strolled into Enlighten, the hotel space for spiritual and healing modalities gaining in popularity such as yoga, meditation, tai chi, EFT and others, combined with a shop filled with books and all kinds of trinkets to aid the seeker's journey. Avery was browsing an aisle filled with candles, incense and other aromatherapy items when he arrived. She was dressed casually in the white tee from the gift bag with Drake Wines emblazoned across the front, black yoga pants that hugged her butt and thighs and white sandals. Her hair was pulled up in a high ponytail. She wore little to no makeup except a clear gloss coating those pillows-for-lips that had haunted his dreams ever since making their acquaintance at First Friday. She pulled in her lower one while studying the trinket-filled shelves. He remembered the taste of wine on them at that first kiss, and the spiciness of her essence he tasted in the storeroom. Something shifted inside him as realization dawned. Avery wanted friendship. Cayden wanted more.

"Good morning, beautiful."

"Good morning, sleepyhead."

Baby steps, but this was the first time their salutatory verbiage had placed them solidly outside of a business relationship.

"Down twenty minutes early? Eager to get going, huh?"

"I'm still on central time. My body thinks it's two hours later." She looked at his long Nike shorts and Jordans. "You're doing yoga in that?"

Cayden shrugged. "I packed for basketball, what can I say."

Avery looked at her watch. "We should get going. I'm excited. Are you excited?"

"Probably not as much as you."

They reached the room listed on their personal itinerary. Cayden opened the door and stepped back for Avery to enter.

"Is this it?" she asked. "The room is smaller than I imagined it would be."

Entering the room, they saw mats, exercise balls, weights and other items—all in sets of two.

"Not many people must have signed up, either. There's only two of everything."

A noise from behind them startled them both. They turned and were surprised to see a petite young woman walk into the room. What they'd thought was a mirror was actually a door.

"Good morning! Welcome to our meditative movement for couples class."

Cayden and Avery looked at each other.

"Good morning," Cayden said. "I'm not sure we're in the right class."

The instructor tapped her phone. "Cayden Barker and Avery Gray?"

Avery nodded. "Yes."

"This is the class that was scheduled. The regular group started about fifteen minutes ago, but if this is a problem, we can hurry and try to get you in."

"What do you think?"

Avery walked over to the bench below the sign requesting that shoes be removed and sat down.

"The time has already been booked for us. I say we go ahead."

"Great! Those were my thoughts exactly. My name is Leann." She pulled a rug from beneath another bench and rolled it out. "Let's get started."

After doing a series of stretches, Leann led them through several moves that required frequent touching and building trust. Partner squats. Sit-ups. Twists. Split lunges. The class that Cayden hadn't been all that thrilled about taking had turned into the best part of his trip so far. She tried not to show it, but he could tell that Avery was into it, too. Forty-five minutes of stretching, pulling, bending and breathing had them both feeling like noodles. All that touching and trust building helped break through the wall of wariness he felt Avery had worn since walking into their suite. She was more playful and flirty—the Avery he most liked.

"What's next?" Avery swayed to music only she could hear while waiting for the elevator.

"Breakfast, and then…do you still want to go horseback riding?"

"It looks fun. Do you?"

"Hell, yeah."

"You ever done it?"

"No."

"Cool. It will be a first for both of us."

The smell of breakfast greeted them at the door of their suite. Gustav explained the menu, inquired of further needs, then bowed and made a discreet exit. Cayden and Avery dined on fluffy pecan waffles, creamy eggs and an assortment of meats and rolls. They showered and changed into jeans, tees and tennis shoes, then obtained a golf cart for their trip to the stables. Their riding instructor was as gentle with them as he was with the horses, and full of information about the fascinating history of the Drakes and more than a thousand lush acres that belonged to them, their expansive resort and the town of Temecula. The trail took over an hour to complete. Both Cayden and Avery fell in love with their horses. As Cayden took in the way Avery's luscious ass filled out those denims, he felt the beginnings of falling in…something…with her, too.

The day flew by and then it was evening. The two dressed to the nines for dinner with the Drakes. All night Cayden admired Avery in her wraparound silk number and stilettos, and imagined how sexy she'd look sans the dress. Donald and Genevieve Drake were delightful, not at all the stuffy, reserved adults their status implied. The outdoor concert that followed dinner capped off a perfect day. Twinkling stars against a sky of midnight blue. Gentle breezes that caressed and teased. Chilled wine and a neo-soul wonder named Janice Baker reminiscent of Lauryn Hill. It all created the perfect atmosphere to stir up wanton desire. A perfect backdrop for love. When the last note ended, they thanked the Drakes for a wonderful evening and returned to the resort.

The car ride was mostly quiet, as was the ride up the elevator and the walk to their suite. Once inside, however, Cayden let his body do the talking. He pulled Avery into his arms and seared her with a kiss. Given her reaction, she didn't mind one bit. Her hands roamed his back as eager fingers played in his curly locks. His hands took a journey down her back to her butt, pressing her into his burgeoning manhood.

He stopped so they could both catch their breath. "I've been wanting to do that all night."

Avery rubbed her breasts against his chest as her hand neared his excitement. "What else would you like to do?"

"I think I can show you better than I can tell you." He reached for the tie on her wraparound dress—and pulled.

Avery's breathy gasp was evidence to how Cayden's move surprised her. That and how one hand did a pitiful job at covering a pair of ripe melons spilling over the lacy bra, while the other performed a lame execution of covering her already-tasted treasure.

His smile was lethal as he reached for her hands. Eyes darkened. Voice lowered.

"Let me see you."

Avery shied away at first but gained confidence as his appreciative eyes roamed the length of her fuchsia-colored, bra-and-panty-covered body. Cayden held her hand and walked behind her. He unclasped her bra. It dropped to the floor. He kissed the back of her neck, the lobe of her ear, as his hands clasped her weighty breasts. His fingers teased the nipples into pebbles of pleasure. He was rewarded with a low moan accompanying her ass rubbing against his crotch.

Cayden was about to burst. But this night was special. He wanted to make it last. He reached down for Avery's dress and wrapped up her curves.

"A glass of champagne?" he asked with the respect of addressing someone who just seconds before was dressed in panties and heels.

Avery's eyes fluttered open. "Wh-what?"

He smiled, gently reaching for her hand and leading them into the dining room. "I think now is the perfect moment to pop the top on Donald's extravagant gift inside the welcoming basket."

Once there he reached into the basket, pulled out a folded blanket and placed it at the edge of the table before lifting Avery and perching her on the soft, fuzzy fabric as though she were made of spun glass.

"What are you doing?"

"Remembering that as amazing as was the dinner presented this evening, I really want a taste of chocolate for dessert."

Avery crossed her arms to cover herself.

Cayden noted the move. "Cold?"

Avery shook her head. "Self-conscious."

"Don't be." He moved her hand and placed his mouth on the nipple it covered. "You look amazing."

He paused only long enough to pull the pricey champagne flutes from their package and retrieve the champagne from the fancy bottle chiller on a nearby table. He popped the cork, filled up both their flutes. They clinked glasses. There was no toast. Cayden felt none was needed. He was getting ready to leave no doubt as to how much he appreciated Avery being there.

"Oh, my goodness!" Avery's eyes sparkled as bursts of flavor snapped, crackled and popped in her mouth. "I think this is the best champagne I've ever tasted."

Cayden's brow raised. "Oh, yeah?"

"Without a doubt."

"Here, taste this."

He took a sip of the brew, then whipped a kiss on Avery hot enough to zap the straight out of her flat-ironed curls.

"How was that?"

"Infinitely better."

He took another sip, French-kissed her nether lips and proceeded to render her to a state of speechlessness. For the next several minutes gasps, hisses and soft mewling sounds were Avery's only means of communication. After licking, kissing and suckling her body into mind-shattering bliss, Cayden quickly sheathed himself and slid his long, thick love sword into the height of her orgasm.

"Ohhhhhhhh…"

"How was that?" he asked, setting up a slow rhythm that suggested he planned to be there awhile.

"So good," Avery managed between pants.

Cayden placed her legs over his shoulders, gripped her hips and plunged to the hilt. For a few seconds he didn't move, just enjoyed the feel of Avery pulsating around him. When he began moving, his hips led the dance—a cross between a tantalizing tango and a slow Alpha Twerk. He was focused, insatiable, propelled the dance from room to room and into the most delicious lovemaking. Avery's body joined in note for note, matching his fervor on the fast grooves, harmonizing on the slow. The sound of pleasure that burst from her when she came again was one of a woman touched in places that had never before known loving could feel like this. Cayden didn't take the time to think about it. He wanted only to bask in Avery and how beautiful it felt to be inside her. Beyond that, in his moment of seismic relief, nothing else mattered.

Eighteen

Avery woke up feeling better than she had in months, all due to the man lying beside her. She lay there taking her internal temperature. What were her feelings the morning after? Guilt? Shame? Frustration? Fear? None of those, much to her surprise. Perhaps it was the affirmations spoken at the end of their couples exercise session yesterday, encouraging one to be present, to live in the moment. Did Cayden feel the same way? She reached for the sheet covering his well-defined chest and began slowly pulling it down to reveal more of his tanned, olive skin. Pausing for a moment, her eyes slid to his face, relaxed and free of creases produced by frowns as he slept. They continued down to his slightly flared nose and the lips that just hours before had performed magic feats. Those memories caused a warm flush to spread across her body. She continued pulling the sheet, exposing the now-languid manhood that had sent her to the moon and around the stars before she'd drifted back down to earth on a cloud of unadulterated bliss. With her target in view, she eased to a sitting position. Fueled by desire and her own wanton thoughts, she repositioned herself closer to his crotch, lifted his penis and kissed it.

Cayden squirmed for just a second before settling back into sleep. But not for long if Avery had her way.

She traced the length of him with her tongue, then pulled him gently into her mouth. A hissing sound suggested Cayden was awake. Seconds later, encouraged by nimble fingers and an eager tongue, his shaft woke up, too. She looked up and into eyes as dark with desire as they were last night. His head fell against the pillow. His hips slowly gyrated. Avery treated his sex like a lollipop in her favorite flavor, savoring every lick. Cayden placed his hand on her head, ran his fingers through her disheveled mane and guided her head as she savored him. His breathing deepened. Movements quickened. He tossed and murmured.

"Oh, baby. Baby! Damn."

She felt he was close to release but for her the party was only beginning. With a final lick and kiss to the tip she reached for one of several gold foils on the bed beside her. Once he was shielded she straddled him, guided his missile to her portal and slowly slid down. She paused as fireworks went off inside her, then set up a lazy rhythm for them both to enjoy. Cayden massaged, licked and kissed her breasts. He palmed her ass and matched her stroke for stroke. It wasn't long before she felt her body reaching its climax. A final thrust. She cried out, went over the edge and collapsed on top of him.

Cayden smoothed hair and tiny beads of sweat away from her forehead. He kissed her temple. "Good morning."

She smiled. "Morning."

"What a wonderful way to wake up."

Avery rolled off Cayden, then cuddled into his side. "You liked that?"

"I loved it."

"I'll keep that in mind." She turned to look outside. "This place is amazing. I could stay here forever."

"I could definitely stay in this bed all day."

"Unfortunately, that's not an option. What time is our flight?"

"Two thirty, but we'll leave here at noon. We're flying commercial from San Diego. Forty-five minutes away."

"In that case I'd better get moving." She climbed out of bed and headed to the en suite. Cayden came up behind her. "Where are you going?"

"To take a shower with you—" he squeezed her cheek "—and get in one more round for the road."

After breakfast and a class in wine making, Cayden and Avery returned to their suite to find their luggage packed and waiting at the door. Avery slept during the limo ride to San Diego and boarded the plane feeling refreshed.

"Thanks again for inviting me here," she said, once they'd gotten settled and the plane took off. "I loved everything about this trip."

Cayden reached for her hand. "What did you love the most?"

Avery gave him a look, then slid her hand toward his crotch. He caught it and folded it into his. "Yes, that was my favorite part, too."

"What happens next?" she asked.

"What do you mean?"

"Was that just vacation sex or…"

"It wasn't just that for me."

"What was it?"

"Why do we have to define it?"

"So that we can both know what to expect." Avery looked out the window at a clear sky that stretched forever. She knew the situation would get tricky with her heart involved. Yet, she hadn't been able to stop it. "Are you dating other people?"

"Not lately. Been too busy."

"You're too yummy for me to get leftovers. I'm not sure I could go the casual route."

"You're the only one on my mind right now. Let's hang out and see what happens."

"I can do that. But let's keep what we're sharing just between us."

Cayden frowned. "Who are we hiding from?"

"You're no longer my client but I still want to be careful. If the good times continue and things get serious, then we can tell the world."

Cayden placed a strong arm around her shoulders and whispered, "As long as we're together, I'll keep my big mouth shut."

Avery chuckled and nestled against him, already anticipating their next good time.

On Monday, she was still smiling. Rather than being exhausted from the whirlwind trip, her whole body hummed with contentment and felt revitalized. The pale yellow suit she chose matched her sunny mood. Her mind was so consumed with thoughts of Cayden she barely remembered the drive from Chicago to the Point. After stopping at the coffee shop, she floated into the office.

The receptionist wasn't at the desk. Charlotte hadn't arrived, either. Avery was surprised to see that Maggie had beat her into work. She placed down her purse and continued on to her boss's office.

"Good morning, Maggie!"

"Good morning."

Avery thought she detected a bit of attitude, but then again, Maggie hadn't been sexed all weekend to within an inch of her life.

"You're here early."

Maggie replied without looking up. "I am."

Okay, there was definitely some 'tude floating around. "Is everything okay?"

"Unfortunately, no." Maggie sighed and put down the report she'd been reading. "Have a seat, Avery. We need to talk."

Avery sat in one of two chairs in front of Maggie's desk. "What about?"

"About you and Cayden Barker."

Avery almost dropped her caramel latte. Had Maggie somehow found out about the trip? Or worse, the storeroom? Until she knew what Maggie knew, Avery played dumb.

"Me and Cayden?"

"Word has it that while handling his golf tournament, you became a bit more than his planner."

"Oh, really." Later, Avery would compliment herself at the show of indignation. "And just who brought you this word?"

"Are you saying it's not true? That your interaction with him was at all times strictly professional?"

"Absolutely."

Maggie's eyes narrowed. "Someone saw the two of

you in exchanges that looked too emotional to be about work. You were both also seen leaving the ballroom and coming here, to the executive offices."

"Everything that happened that weekend was related to work."

"Even what took place in one of the empty offices?"

The question raised Avery's back off the chair. She inwardly flinched as her mind raced with questions of her own. *Who saw? Who told? Were there cameras?* That day was seared into memory—the faces of who she encountered from the time she arrived at work Friday morning until dragging home after the banquet and dance that night. Vanessa. Charlotte. Chef Lamar. Those were the first faces that came to mind. But there were others. Teagan. Brittany. Had they greased a club employee's palm and loosened their tongue? Avery's heart sank.

"Well?" When Avery didn't respond, Maggie continued. "The rules clearly state that there is no associating with Point Country Club clients outside of a professional capacity. I emphasized that point during our interview."

Avery knew she should say something. Her mind and mouth all of a sudden seemed to be keeping different hours.

"You know, Avery—"

"It was offered as a kind gesture. I should not have accepted. Cayden—"

Maggie's brow raised.

"Mr. Barker knew I'd been working hard. He thought I needed to eat and set it up…"

What happened in itself was problematic. Saying the words out loud sounded twice as bad.

"I shouldn't have humored him by having lunch. He was—is—a valuable client bringing some of the most important people in the world to our club for the weekend. You stressed what an exceptional opportunity it was to have members of SOMA here. I made an exception."

Every word Avery had spoken was true. She held Maggie's gaze.

Maggie shook her head as she reached for a pen. "You had an incredibly bad lapse in judgment, Avery. I get your reasoning. SOMA's huge. It was only lunch. If it were only up to me, given the circumstances, I may have made the same call. But it's not just me—the board's rules are very clear and you're on probation. I'll have to report this."

"I understand."

"Until they've responded, I'm sorry but I'll have to put you on unpaid administrative leave. Please gather your personal items and turn in your keys."

Fifteen minutes later, a numb Avery carried a small box to the trunk of her car, got in and pulled out of the lot. Thinking of Cayden, she tapped the phone icon. Her call went to voice mail.

Getting my dream man may cost me my dream job. All the way home, she pondered the irony.

Nineteen

Cayden worked to remain calm as he sat in the plush New York executive offices of Elite Bank and Trust, a privately owned institution with dozens of branches along the east coast. His sales staff had done wonders in getting the AI Interface software placed in the top ten office and computer stores throughout the country. If he enjoyed even a fraction of the unparalleled success that was possible, in the span of five years he'd be a billionaire. It was a rare moment when both his personal and professional life was going gangbusters. Maybe a first. Which reminded him to return Avery's call. She'd phoned last night just as he'd arrived at a restaurant to have dinner with a group of SOMA members in the banking industry that he'd met during the golf tournament. He pulled out his phone to send her a text and realized she'd called again.

"Mr. Barker?" He looked up. An attractive, impeccably dressed older woman walked toward him.

He stood. "Yes?"

"Mr. Broadeaux will see you now."

Cayden dashed off a quick Call you later text to Avery while following the woman from the lobby to the grand corner offices of Oliver Broadeaux, located on the building's fifty-seventh floor.

"May I get you something to drink?" she asked. "Coffee, tea, soda, water…"

"I'm fine. Thank you."

She opened a set of double doors. A short entryway with an antique-looking table holding a bouquet of fresh cut flowers flowed into an L-shaped room where natural light flowed from windows on three sides.

"Mr. Broadeaux," his assistant announced with what Cayden felt was unnecessary pomp and circumstance, "I present Mr. Barker."

Oliver Broadeaux was a balding man of average height and giant personality, a beer gut testing the limits of the black suit coat he wore and the white shirt beneath it. He stood and came from behind his desk. Everything about him and the room reeked with an odor of understated wealth.

"Providing the highest quality service and information available for your client has never been easier than with this software," Cayden segued after brief pleasantries. "Once it catches on, the financial services industries will never be the same."

Two hours and a catered lunch later, Cayden left the building a happy man. There was still paperwork to process and numbers to crunch but Oliver had signed on to have AI Interface installed on every computer in every

Elite Bank from New York to Florida. Even more, he'd promised to put in a good word to a friend and golfing buddy whose family owned the largest bank chain in the United States. Achieving that billionaire status was looking more achievable by the minute. He couldn't wait to share the good news. After texting his location to the car service, he pulled out his phone and redialed Avery.

"Hey, babe. Sorry about just now getting back with you. I had to fly to New York for back-to-back meetings. It's been crazy but I've got great news!"

A second and then, "What's that?"

Cayden's brow creased. She'd gone for chipper, but he heard stressed.

"Wait. Is everything okay? Are you all right?"

"We can talk about me later. What's your good news?" She did a better job that time.

"I landed the first major client for AI Interface."

"Cayden, that's great. Who is it?"

"Elite Bank and Trust, one of the largest private banks on the east coast."

"I believe I've seen them. Do they have a branch in Orlando?"

"They have about thirty branches throughout that state alone. Next year they're expanding into the Midwest, with my software on every manager's computer in every branch."

"I'm really happy for you, Cayden. And proud of you, too."

"Enough about me and these millions and billions I'm about to make. What's going on that has you trying your best to sound happy when you're really not?"

"Maggie found out about what happened in the storeroom. I've been put on unpaid administrative leave."

Cayden stopped moving. Sound faded away.

"Cayden?"

"I don't want to say that I heard you, but I think I did." His car pulled to the curb. He got in. "How?" And then another thought that almost stopped Cayden's heart. "Were there cameras?"

"I thought that, too, and almost died. But I asked maintenance and thankfully no, there are no cameras in that room."

"Then how did she find out?"

"Someone who saw us together reported it."

"And she fired you?"

"The rules forced her to put me on leave until the board meets. Being with a client outside of a professional capacity is not allowed."

"Damn." Cayden watched the Manhattan hustle bustle as the car stutter-stepped down Park Avenue. "Whatever you're going to do, whatever you need, I'm here for you, okay?"

"I'm still too stunned to do anything."

"Don't worry about it. We've got this. Hey, since you're not at the club right now, do we still have to be on the DL?"

"Totally. If the universe is granting miracles, I might get to keep my job. If not, the gossip mills will swing wide open with all eyes on me. They're probably cracked already."

"Then come up with where you want me to take you this weekend. Just text the city. I'll handle everything else."

Cayden ended the call; the need to protect Avery he'd

felt almost from the moment they met grew stronger than ever. He no longer had to decide whether or not he wanted a serious relationship. He realized he was in one.

Twenty

The universe must have been fresh out of miracles. The board met. She was officially terminated. Yet here, a month later, Avery caught herself humming. *When did I start doing that?* Didn't matter when it started. She knew the reason why—Cayden. He's why she could hum and smile after being fired from her dream job, turning down positions that did not fit her goals and having her résumé rejected from several businesses she may have considered. Thankfully, a wise portfolio and prudent financial planning had put her in a position to be selective in her choice. The time off had given her an opportunity to invest quality time in a relationship. This had been a learning experience for both of them, about each other and themselves. They spent most of their time outside Point du Sable, with Cayden often chartering planes for quick jaunts to nearby Kansas City, Atlanta, Memphis and Detroit. They spent almost a week in New York—Cayden handing Avery his black card for her to get "whatever" while, after finalizing the AI Interface deal, he held a two-day training session with more than a dozen of Elite Bank and Trust's regional managers. Together they took in a private art exhibit in Tribeca, fabulous dinners, a performance of the Harlem Repertory Theatre. But mostly once his business was done, the two handled business of their own. Alone. Naked. On fire. Cayden had pulled out Avery's inner freak!

The memories alone warmed her body as she placed two bags of groceries in the trunk and got in her car for the short drive to Lisa's house. She'd just secured her seat belt when there was a tap on her window. She turned, sighed and pressed a button.

"Brittany."

"So you do remember me."

"I meant to call. I've been busy."

"So I've heard."

This got Avery's attention. Brittany had grown up in Point du Sable, knew almost everybody. Had she somehow learned what happened and put the fraternizing bug in Maggie's ear?

She crossed her arms. "What exactly have you heard, Brittany?"

"That you're working at the country club, of course. But from your reaction, you imagined something else."

Avery's eyes narrowed. "You knew I worked there."

"I thought you'd been contracted. It wasn't until running into Bruce a week or so later that I learned otherwise."

Bruce. Cayden's friend from Northwestern. Teagan's

date. This revelation provided more questions than answers and didn't narrow Avery's whodunit list one bit.

"That's a very prestigious position, Avery. Congratulations."

Brittany sounded sincere but could no longer be trusted; that Avery was fired, moot. "Thank you."

"I ran into Lisa the other day. She probably told you. I could tell from her reaction that how I fled the scene without a word hurt her as much as it did you."

Speaking of Lisa... "That was a long time ago," Avery answered, starting the car. "We've all moved on."

Brittany placed a hand on the car door. "I don't know if you heard but my marriage is over. I'm not sure if my move back is permanent but, while here, I could sure use a friend."

"Take care of yourself, Brittany." Avery put the car in gear. "I've got to go."

During the short drive from the grocery store to Lisa's house, Avery thought about her friendship with Brittany. How she'd been so ready to help the older girl expose Cayden's illicit activities—confident that it was the right thing to do. But was it? Had he been vindicated because of his Eddington connection, as Avery had believed, or because of his innocence, as Lisa had claimed? Avery knew this was something she had to find out...and soon.

She didn't see much of Cayden for the next two weeks. Most of his time was spent in New York. Avery set up a website and planned for the clients she'd already booked—a bachelorette party and a woman celebrating the big five-o. Both were in December, with holiday themes. When Cayden invited her to meet him on Friday, at what sounded like a quaint cabin in the midst of a forest, she actually got goose bumps. Cayden said he was excited, too. The time spent apart gave them time to miss each other. Plus, she'd finally get to ask him about those embezzlement charges and why they were dropped.

They spent that Friday night and most of Saturday in bed. That afternoon, they channeled their inner B. Smith and tackled a dinner that included a blueberry cake. The dinner digestif, a Drake Wines pecan and vanilla-flavored liqueur that Donald had sent him, was enjoyed during a bubble bath in a high-tech spa tub with built-in sound, colored lights and silent jets.

"Let me taste it," Cayden said, making lazy eights across Avery's stomach and easing farther down.

She snuggled against his soapy chest. "You're drinking the same thing."

"I want to taste it on your lips."

He did, for about five minutes.

"I didn't know whether or not I'd like this," Avery cooed, spreading her legs to give Cayden easier access. "But you've made me a believer."

Much later, they lay in bed completely satisfied. Cayden lazily stroked Avery's hair as they stared out of the glass ceiling above the floating mattress.

"I have an idea."

"Hmm."

"The chamber of commerce is giving me some type of award for the AI Interface invention and the Society's ongoing contribution to fighting and preventing cancer. Come to the dinner with me."

"Really, Cayden? Congratulations!"

"So you'll come?"

"Sure, why not?"

Cayden turned on his side and pulled Avery against him. "You're starting to grow on me, you know that?"

"I do now."

Cayden slid his tongue in her mouth and a finger down the crevice of her backside. His ardent lovemaking made her forget all about the embezzlement question, and everything else.

That Saturday evening, Avery pulled into the drive of the Point Country Club behind a line of limos and luxury cars. The initial plan had been for her to meet Cayden at his house but a busted pipe in the condo above hers leaked water into her unit, requiring a plumber and delaying her plans. She'd phoned Cayden, explained what happened and said she'd meet him there.

It was her first time on the club grounds since being terminated. Almost immediately, she ran into Maggie, who seemed genuinely glad to see her. Cayden was standing with a group of guys, looking *GQ* in a steel-gray tuxedo. He broke away as soon as he saw her and walked over. The hug was brief, his body rigid.

"Are you all right?"

"Better now." He reached for her hand and managed a smile. "Come on. There's some people I want you to meet."

He placed her arm in his and walked back over to the group of men. Three were Eddingtons—Derrick, Dwight and Jake. The other was Bob Masters, who she remembered from Cayden's fundraiser. The subdued gentleman before her was nothing like the gregarious man she'd met that night. Did Bob have something to do with Cayden's tense demeanor?

The two entered the club. For the remainder of the cocktail hour, Avery and Cayden separated to work the room. Avery distributed several of her newly designed business cards offering her freelance services. Dinner was sublime. Halfway through it, the ceremony began. The mayor welcomed everyone. A local teenager sang the national anthem. Last year, the talented girl tagged as "the small body with a big voice" had taken third place on a national reality-TV talent competition show. When Cayden was recognized as one of five businesspersons of the year and named Shining Star of Point du Sable, Avery couldn't have been prouder. That he included her in his brief acceptance speech as a critical key to his fundraiser's success made her heart swell.

"Did you have a good time?" Cayden asked as they said their goodbyes to friends and peers and prepared to leave.

"It was a wonderful evening. Great for networking. I enjoyed myself."

"Any potential new clients?"

"I gave out a lot of cards. We'll see. What about you?"

"Honestly, I've had better evenings."

"What happened?"

Cayden's eyes shifted. "Tell you later."

Avery followed his line up sight and almost lost her dinner. The last person in the world she needed to see that night came toward her with arms outstretched.

"Avery!"

"Hello, Brittany."

Avery endured rather than returned the hug. There was enough saccharin in that fake greeting to cause diabetes. So as not to ruin what had been a nice evening, she was cordial.

Brittany turned to Cayden. "Hey, stranger."

"Britt." Cayden didn't get the cordial memo. "Excuse us. We're on our way out."

"I know. I almost missed you. I wanted to congratulate you on the award and tell you how impressed I am that your heart is big enough to forgive those who've wronged you."

"I forgave you, Brittany, for my own peace of mind. Forgiving isn't forgetting. Point is a small town but if you're back here to stay I hope it's one large enough for us to have very limited interaction. Excuse us."

"I wasn't talking about me," Brittany said as Cayden began to walk past her. "I'm talking about Avery."

A sense of foreboding slowly crawled up Avery's spine. She gently prodded Cayden. "Let's just go."

He'd already turned around. "What about Avery?"

"Oh, you don't know?" Brittany's smug look shifted from Cayden to Avery. "Don't worry, sistah. Once upon a time, you had my back. Tonight—" she winked "—I've got yours."

"What's this? A minireunion?" Lawrence Kincaid sidled over and slid an arm around Brittany's waist. "Wish we could stay and shoot the breeze, but we have an early flight."

"The Seychelles," Brittany added, then looked pointedly at Avery. "That's near Africa."

"Aren't search engines wonderful?" Avery replied. She felt Cayden reach for her hand. "Safe travels."

Avery imagined a scenario where Cayden let pass what Brittany had said. But the way he was holding—almost crushing—her hand suggested otherwise.

Twenty-One

"What in the hell was that about?" Cayden's low tone and casual expression belied the anger that emanated from his body as he walked beside her.

She understood. There were eyes on them, some no doubt who'd witnessed the tense exchange. For one of the night's honorees to get into an all-out brouhaha would not be a good look.

"Brittany is being her usual messy self." She tried to sound unaffected and was almost successful. "Cayden, my hand."

He loosened his grip. She relaxed her face into a small smile and made sure to look at and acknowledge those they passed outside.

"Is it too late for a drive into Chicago to see the lights?" she asked.

"Yes."

Avery swallowed, and hoped he was only answering the question she'd asked.

They reached the valet booth. While waiting for his Porsche to be pulled around, after getting into the car and during the short drive from the country club to a residence just outside the Estates that Avery assumed was Cayden's house, he didn't say a word.

"You live here?"

"No. I thought it would be a good idea to park in a stranger's drive."

She noticed he wouldn't look at her. Not a good sign. Avery began to get a bad feeling. Shoulda, woulda and coulda rushed by for a chat.

He'll believe me. After I explain that I didn't know the envelope's contents, he'll understand.

"Earlier, you asked if everything was all right."

This was about Bob, not Brittany. *Wasn't it?* Avery took a breath. "Yes, I was worried about you."

"Bob hit me with some pretty tough news," he continued, staring straight ahead. "Said the review board had hit a snag in my vetting process."

Avery worked to swallow past the rapidly expanding lump in her throat. "They did?"

"They want to look deeper into the embezzlement allegations from my youth, into the lies Brittany told as revenge for my leaving her. He doesn't know if I'll be confirmed."

"Cayden, I'm so sorry." Avery had no other words.

Finally, he looked at Avery, lifted a brow in a scowl that was as Oscar-worthy as it was hot. "You and Brittany were friends back then. Were you involved?"

He seemed not to breathe as he awaited her answer.

"It's complicated."

"That's a yes or no question."

"It's yes and no. Cayden, please, can't we go inside to have this conversation?"

"No." She imagined Lawrence's words from the First Friday spat taunted him. "What did Brittany mean back there?"

Avery sighed, swallowed hard. "One day Brittany called and asked for a favor; said she wasn't feeling good and needed something delivered to her job."

His eyes widened ever so slightly. "So, she wasn't lying."

She turned to him. "Technically, no, but she didn't tell the whole truth, either."

His hands gripped the steering wheel. "Did you or did you not give the reports she'd doctored to her manager?"

"I did, but—"

"That's all I needed to know."

"I had no idea what the report was about!"

His snort and side glance suggested he didn't buy it.

"Did you believe what the papers reported? That I was guilty of theft?"

"She was my friend. Lisa's, too. I barely knew you, and believed what she told me."

"I've heard enough." He started the car.

"Cayden, no." She placed a hand on his forearm. "Not before I have a chance to explain."

He shook off her hand. "What part of 'I've heard enough' don't you understand?" He jerked the car into gear and roared down the drive.

Avery's spirit fell. She knew he was angry and had a temper. She'd witnessed it before, the night of the ball. That didn't mean he had the right to treat her with such disregard. If he didn't think enough of her to hear her side of the story, then she'd gladly leave him to stew alone. The silence howled from his driveway back to the country club. Through the glass she could see a few stragglers but thankfully no sign of Brittany, who Avery was sure would like nothing more than to rub more dirt in her face. Cayden pulled up to the valet and stared straight ahead.

"Cayden," she began softly, her hand on the handle.

He abruptly got out of the car, walked around to her door and opened it. She raised her hand toward him, silently forcing him to assist her. Once out of the car, with another couple nearby, she placed an affectionate hand on his arm, produced a smile she didn't feel and whispered, "I'm so sorry, Cayden. I should have told you sooner. I meant to, several times."

He matched her act with his own, put a hand on her shoulder and with cold eyes and a warm smile responded.

"Goodbye."

Avery used the act of fishing out her valet ticket to bat away tears. He didn't actually add "and good riddance," but from his tone he might as well have.

Twenty-Two

On the way home and all day Sunday, the act of Avery's betrayal replayed in his head. On Sunday night, he accepted Jake's invite to meet up with the guys for a game of basketball, the perfect outlet for the energy pent up inside him. On Monday, he placed the hurt, disappointment, anger and, yes, heartbreak into a nice, tight mental compartment and locked it up. He forced away all thoughts of Avery. Though the pace of interest and orders for AI Interface had slowed due to Labor Day weekend, he worked ten-hour days, worked out in the club gym until exhaustion claimed him, grabbed a bite to eat before going to bed, then got up and repeated the schedule. The following Saturday, his phone rang early. Roused out of sleep, his first thought was uncensored.

Avery?

No, his mother. "Yes, my name is Tami. I'm wondering if you can help me locate my son?"

Cayden flopped on his back. "Hi, Mom."

"He lives!"

"Sorry about not getting back with you. I've been busy."

"We're nearing Labor Day weekend. I thought work would slow down."

"It will, in a couple more weeks. How are you doing?"

"Busy, as well, thanks largely to the donation from your fundraiser. We've had a steady stream of new patients from other hospitals referred to our specialists. That they have access to previously unavailable treatment...it makes me very proud."

"Thanks, Mom."

"I know you're this award-winning superstar and all—"

"Stop it."

"When am I going to get to see you?"

"What are you doing today?"

"Working until five."

"How about you Uber to work and I'll pick you up there for dinner."

"You've got a date."

"See you then."

Cayden slept in, surfed the TV and web and ran errands. At forty thirty, he pulled into PDS Medical's emergency parking lot. He'd purposely come early to see his mom in action, maybe get introduced to someone benefiting from the program. He waved to a couple people he recognized before reaching the nurse's station.

"I know you," the cute redhead chirped.

"Anyone would," said the older woman standing

behind the redhead reading a chart through bifocaled glasses. "He looks just like his mom."

Redhead stayed focused on Cayden. "Maybe, but haven't I seen you in the paper a few times?"

"It's possible," Cayden said.

"Cayden!" Tami checked her watch as she rounded the corner. "You're early."

"I know. Thought I'd make a round or two with you."

"That's nice but not possible. You can, however, come to the office. I have some paperwork to wrap up."

"I was hoping to speak with someone who's benefited from our program."

"We'd have to get their permission beforehand. Patient confidentiality and all that jazz."

A pretty woman with short black hair and warm brown eyes smiled when she saw Tami.

"Leaving so soon?" Tami teased.

"Not soon enough!"

"Lisa, this is my son—"

"Cayden. He knows me from high school. I'm Avery's sister."

"Who's Avery?" Tami asked, looking from Cayden to Lisa.

"Lisa's sister," Cayden responded. He saw a dare in Lisa's eyes as he extended his hand. "Nice to see you again, Lisa. It's been a long time."

"Since the two of you obviously know each other why don't you catch up while I finish up work? Son, I'll meet you in the lobby. Lisa, you look radiant. I'm so happy you're better."

"Me, too." They hugged. Tami disappeared down the hall. Lisa eyed Cayden. "Can we sit for a chat?"

"Do I want to?"

"Probably not but that would probably be easier than me making a scene."

He smirked but fell in step as she walked to a nearby set of chairs.

"Avery told me what happened," Lisa began before sitting down.

Cayden sat one chair over. "Then what's left to say?"

"Look, it's not my business but you're way off course here. Brittany lied to me the same as Avery. She was very convincing, even produced tears while lamenting how she'd put in a good word to get you hired, only to have you not only break up with her but steal from the bank. She was like a best friend to me. I had no idea she could be that vengeful and manipulative. Avery trusted her because she was my friend. She used my sister because she could. Again, it's not my business. But if the look on my sister's face after returning from California is any indication, the two of you were on your way to something special. You're old enough to know that doesn't happen every day. Again, it's not my business and I know I'm biased, but if you're going to pronounce a woman guilty and kick her to the curb, you should at least do so after hearing her defense."

"Are you an attorney?"

"Close. A big sister."

Cayden saw where Avery got some of her feistiness and couldn't help but smile. "How do you know my mom?"

"During chemotherapy, she was my nurse."

"Ah, yes. Avery told me you were a patient here."

"Through the initial diagnosis and six weeks of treatment. Now I'm only back every two weeks for checkups. Once a month if the next exam comes back okay."

"I never thought to ask my mom if she knew you. The world is even smaller than I thought."

Lisa's phone rang. She stood. "Gotta take this. It's my daughter. Hello, baby, hang on." She muted the call and looked at Cayden, who'd stood, as well. "Avery isn't perfect. But she's honest, kind and a little too trusting. There are two sides to every story. If you ever cared anything about her at all, she'll get the chance to tell you hers."

Without so much as a wave or a goodbye, Lisa waltzed down the hall and out of Emergency's double doors. Cayden was still standing when Tami came up behind him.

"All right, son, ready? I hope so. I'm starved."

Cayden walked out of the hospital with Tami, still spinning from Hurricane Lisa. For the past week he'd been able to not think about Avery. Big sis had put her smack-dab back on his mind.

It wasn't her first breakup. They hadn't dated long. Could what they'd experienced be called a relationship at all? The more Avery thought about the past several weeks, the more she realized that they'd both engaged in a whirlwind fantasy of unrealistic and unsustainable euphoria that was bound to come crashing down at some point. Wasn't that what had happened every other time she'd taken a chance on love? Scenes from their non-stop good times played like a video in her mind. Visiting the Charles H. Wright and Motown museums in Detroit. Messily eating ribs slathered in sauce with their fingers while enjoying traditional jazz on KC's 18th and Vine. Front row seats and backstage passes to Rihanna in Atlanta. Making love on a Malibu beach under a full moon. Lots of extravagant dinners and decadent sex.

Sharing dreams and celebrating victories. Avery had floated through these amazing experiences high on love. A week or two more of that life and she would have believed in happily-ever-after.

But the night they went public with their romance, confirming the gossipy whispers blowing over the Point, reality had made an ugly appearance. In less than five minutes, Brittany Moore-Wellington had erased two months of ecstasy by opening her big mouth. With one sentence she'd stomped her feet all over Avery's sandcastle. It was foolish to think Cayden could ever forget what he perceived as her betrayal. Especially since it involved another woman who'd done him wrong. She'd hoped that after calming down he would at least take her calls. It had been two weeks since the banquet and still Cayden was radio silent. Not talking to him was tearing her up inside. If she couldn't have his forever, she'd settle for forgiveness. In order for her to move on, Avery at least needed that.

Feeling a modicum of control for the first time since the big reveal, Avery walked over to where her phone lay on the bar counter. She plugged "Eddington Enterprise" into the search engine, then tapped the phone icon to place a call.

"Good morning, Eddington Enterprise. How may I direct your call?"

"Jake Eddington."

"Who may I say is calling?"

Avery considered shielding her identity. But only for a nanosecond. If Cayden's friends were also not talking, best to know now. Not being truthful is how she got here.

"Avery Gray."

"One moment!"

The receptionist's cheery voice did little to quell her nervousness. What if he chose not to take her call? Like Cayden, Jake was a grown man. She couldn't force him to talk. Avery paced the room. After her third time around the living space, she decided to end the call. Just as her thumb hovered over the phone's face, he answered.

"Eddington."

"Jake?"

"Yes, this is Jake. Hi, Avery."

"Hi. I was beginning to think you wouldn't take my call."

"I was on the other line."

"Oh, okay. I'm sure you know why I'm calling."

"I wouldn't want to assume. Why don't you tell me."

"It's about Cayden. He won't return my calls."

"And you're calling me because…?"

"Because I believe the two of you are close, he's being an insensitive jerk and I thought if you hit him upside the head hard enough during one of those pickup basketball games, you just might be able to knock some sense into him!"

Avery totally did not mean for all of that to come out but once the words began spilling out, she couldn't stop them. When she finished, Jake laughed so hard he put a smile on her face.

"I'm sorry. I've been holding that in for two weeks and once I opened my mouth…"

"The lava flowed, huh?"

"Ha! The lava flowed. He's doing okay, though?"

"Seems fine. Doesn't mean it's true. Men hide their feelings."

"Women erupt."

"You said that."

"I can't believe how much I said."

"Listen, Cayden's my friend and I'm not one to get in the middle of another couple's situation. I will tell you that what happened with Brittany all those years ago definitely scarred him. It's hard to gain his trust, and if ever broken it's hard to get it back."

"Did he tell you what happened?"

"Not in detail."

"He thinks I plotted with Brittany. It wasn't like that at all. I had no idea that what I thought was a favor to her would have a negative impact on him."

"Did you tell him that?"

"I tried, the night it happened. He wouldn't listen then and now won't take my calls."

"I can't change that, Avery. He's an adult."

"Can you at least tell him that I called and asked about him and that I would still like to explain exactly what happened?"

"Why is that so important to you, if you don't mind me asking?"

"Because Cayden isn't the only one who's trust has been betrayed. I know that feeling and it sucks. Which is why I'd never do that to anyone I care about. I'm not Brittany. My reputation matters. I'd prefer that Cayden cut ties based on truth, rather than stay angry based on a lie."

"I like you, Avery." She could hear the smile in his voice. "I'll give Cayden your message."

"Thank you."

Avery fell back against the couch, exhausted and relieved. She'd said to Jake what she couldn't say to Cayden. The next move, if there was one, would be on him.

Twenty-Three

Cayden was nervous to the point of almost being physically ill. Bob had called and asked to see him right away. The Society of Ma'at conference was held two weeks ago, but as of last week when he'd questioned Bob about the results, he said final decisions hadn't come down. All the way from his home to Bob's house, which was on the other side of Point du Sable's downtown, Cayden tried to imagine what had come of the board's investigation. Had they confirmed the truth of his innocence and made a decision? By the time he arrived and rang the doorbell, he still hadn't figured it out.

Bob opened the door. He wasn't smiling.

Cayden covered his fear with bravado. "Mr. Masters! Good to see you."

Bob nodded but remained somber. "Come on in, son."

Two steps in and Cayden's world went black. A hood

had been thrown over his head. He was being corralled by what felt like two or three men on all sides of him. Wrestling against their vicelike grip was useless.

"Hey, let go of me! What's going on? Mr. Masters? Bob!"

As they wrangled him down a flight of stairs, Cayden realized that either he was being kidnapped for a ransom his mother, Tami, couldn't possibly pay, or he was being initiated into the überexclusive fraternal order of the Society of Ma'at.

It was the latter. Cayden Barker was a Society man! Later that night, he was invited to the Estates for a dinner attended by only SOMA men. There were pats on the back and hearty congratulations. He received his SOMA ring. It was a milestone he'd dared not put on his bucket list, yet the impossible had happened before he'd turned thirty. He was in a room filled with powerful, successful men of integrity who believed he belonged there. In a rare moment of nostalgia, Cayden thought about the father he could barely remember, the one who left when he was five. His thoughts drifted to someone else, too. Avery. They hadn't talked for over a month. He missed her. Over the past couple days, his anger had subsided. He'd begun to allow his mind to consider what his heart already knew. What Jake, Lisa and even Avery had tried to tell him. She hadn't known what was in the envelope. Unlike Brittany, she told the truth. He wanted to leave right then to speak with her but being the guest of honor that wouldn't be cool. So he smiled and joked through dessert, cigars and brandy before thanking his new brothers for taking time from their busy schedules to welcome him into the family. When he headed toward the door, Jake fell in beside him.

"What's going on?"

"About what?"

"Whatever had your attention for the second half of the evening. What does that song say? Your body was here but your mind was on the other side of town."

Was he that transparent? "You're tripping."

"Am I? Or are you finally coming to your senses about Avery, and almost ready to give her another chance. Or a phone call at the very least."

They reached the set of doors leading to the parking area.

"You think you know everything, don't you?"

"Pretty much." Jake opened the door, then followed Cayden outside. "So when are you going to call her?"

"Man, get some business."

"You are my business."

"Whatever." They reached Cayden's Porsche. Cayden turned to give Jake a shoulder hug. "I appreciate what you guys did for me tonight."

"You deserve everything, man. You've earned it."

"Thanks again, bro." Cayden slid into the velvety leather seat and started the car.

"Call Avery!" Jake threw up a wave, but Cayden had sped away.

As he left Bob's house, he tapped the steering wheel to engage his phone. For several weeks, Avery's number had occupied a top spot on the digital Rolodex screen that listed people based on number of calls. That he had to say her name was telling. It had been a long time since they talked. Cayden reached the main road. After sitting there for several seconds, he canceled placing a call, bypassed his home and hit the interstate on the way to Chicago. A conversation with Avery was long overdue. He hoped she was home.

With twenty minutes to think about it, Cayden changed his mind about a surprise visit. He didn't have the right to bum-rush her like that. They hadn't spoken in over a month. What if she'd moved on? As long as it had taken to make up his mind, Cayden decided, the move would serve him right. He pulled into a corner gas station and tapped Avery's number. The sound of her ringing phone reverberated through him. That she didn't want to take his call or talk with him was something else he hadn't thought about. Her answering machine kicked in. He didn't leave a message. After idling in the gas lane for a minute, weighing his limited options, he put the car in gear and headed toward the exit that would put him in the proper lane to turn right and enter the interstate on-ramp. Just before he exited the gas station, his phone rang.

"Hello, Avery."

"Cayden."

Defensive. Guarded. He understood.

"It's been a while since we've talked."

Silence. She wasn't going to make it easy.

"Look, if this is about Lisa and what hap—"

"I'm glad Lisa did what she did. But this isn't about that. I wanted to see you, to have the conversation now that you wanted to have back then. At the time, I was too upset to listen to anything you had to say, or what anyone else said for that matter. But I've had time to cool off, take a step back and analyze the whole situation and… it wasn't fair of me to cut things off without us having a real conversation. That's why I'm calling. If you're open to it, I'd really appreciate getting together."

"I could do that."

"Good. How about now?"

"It's late."

"This doesn't have to take long. I'll understand if you can't see me tonight, but I don't want to wait. We had some amazing times together, Avery. If after meeting we go our separate ways, then okay. But I do have a few things I'd like to say to you."

"I don't want to argue."

"Me, either."

A pause and then, "Where are you?"

"In the city, actually, not too far from your neighborhood. Where are you?"

"At Kaphraos."

Cayden smiled at the irony. He'd passed her on the way to Chicago. The Thai restaurant, a take-out favorite, was less than ten minutes from his house. "Is it possible for me to meet you there in, say, twenty minutes? Can you wait?"

"Okay."

A car Cayden hadn't noticed was behind him beeped his horn. Cayden pressed the accelerator, veered onto the on-ramp and unleashed the Porsche's horses. A drive that should have taken at least twenty minutes was done in ten.

He walked into Kaphraos and scanned the tables. She half stood and waved. Cayden thought she looked thinner than he remembered. The devilish glint in her eyes when she'd tease him had been replaced by wariness. Her expression gave nothing away. Had he done that?

Once at the table, he offered a genuine smile. How much he'd missed her was evident in how rapidly his heart beat now. He wanted to hug her. That might be pre-sumptuous. But considering where his lips had touched her body, a handshake seemed far too formal.

He removed his coat and sat down. "Hey there."

"Hi."

"Thanks for waiting."

She nodded. "No problem."

"You dining alone tonight?"

"Lisa and the fam had just left when you called."

Cayden noticed the friendly server who often waited on him about to come over. He shook his head just enough to halt her steps. His gaze returned to Avery's face. His heart dropped from the hurt that he saw there.

"Avery, baby, I'm truly sorry for how everything went down."

He hadn't meant to use the affectionate term. It slipped out. But seeing how her face softened and her shoulders relaxed, he was glad it happened.

She lowered her eyes. "I'm sorry, too."

"I wish I'd handled the situation differently. When Brittany accused you of helping in her scheme, I was blindsided—shocked, angry, confused. We're talking about the worst time in my life. My character was called into question, reputation almost ruined, career nearly de-railed. In that moment and for weeks afterward, there was nothing you could have done or said to me that would have excused what you did or made a difference in how I felt.

"Understand, I was a seventeen-year-old snot-nosed kid when Brittany and I got together. She was the older woman—experienced, worldly, very manipulative.

Wanted to get married. I didn't. At all. She responded by trying to destroy my life."

"She did that to a lot of us."

"How? What did she say that made you want to help her destroy me?"

"That was never my intention, Cayden. Please believe me on that." Avery removed her coat. "It's true that the way Brittany described you seemed nothing like the cute guy I used to ogle on the basketball court."

That comment brought their first shared smile.

"As you just said, Brittany can be very deceitful and manipulative. But the way she framed what she told me and Lisa, *you* were being those things. She played the victim to perfection. Even so, when she asked me to deliver that envelope to her manager, I had no idea what it contained."

Cayden noticed the server for their station watching them. He motioned her over, then asked Avery, "Are you hungry?"

"Finishing up dinner is why I was here late."

"Cool. What would you like to drink?"

Avery ordered a Thai-spiced hot chocolate. Cayden opted for a decaf Black Thai, made with coffee, tea and evaporated milk. Neither of them touched the menus the server placed down.

"You didn't find it strange that she'd involve you in her work?"

"I thought I was doing a friend a favor. Later, she told me you'd used her, that you'd dated her in order to steal from the bank and then broke up with her when she threatened to speak out. Later still, when she finally told me what I'd given her manager, I felt I'd helped to prevent a crime and done the right thing."

"And when I was exonerated?"

"Still thought you were guilty, I'm embarrassed to say. Thought the Eddingtons' clout and money had gotten you off."

"That, and not my good looks?"

"If the prosecuting attorney was female, that would have totally worked."

Cayden sat back, absorbing what Avery told him, which was similar to what Lisa shared when she cornered him in the hospital. A month ago, he would have had trouble buying the story. But having had time to reflect on Brittany's skillful machinations, he could now accept what Avery told him as truth.

"It's why I wanted so desperately to speak with you," Avery continued. "I could only imagine how this all appeared in your mind and how, given how close we'd become and all we'd shared, it felt like a second betrayal. But it wasn't. In getting to know you I felt that the man you'd become looked nothing like the one who the town thought had hacked through Brittany's account to steal money from the bank. May I ask you something?"

"Anything."

"Why didn't you fight back? Reveal what was really going on when it happened?"

"I cleared my name to those who mattered. Once the situation was rectified, I was advised to quickly put it behind me and focus on my career. Meanwhile Brittany came to understand that leaving town was in her best interest."

"Why?"

"Because after I hired a detective *for real*, it was proven that she was the one who'd been embezzling from her employer. The bank president was friends with her family and demanded restitution but decided not to prosecute."

"But what about you? Why didn't you sue her for slander? She had everyone believing you were a thief!"

"There were retractions in the local and regional papers, but as often happens, they were placed in near obscurity instead of on the front page where my story ran. I was a rising star at Eddington Enterprise. Derrick wanted it over, to get the company out of that type of spotlight. Monamama said karma would take care of the rest."

"Mona who?"

Cayden laughed. "Jake's mother. As my pseudo-adopted mom, that's what I came up with."

"Cute." They paused while the server delivered their drinks. "Where do we go from here?"

"I'd like to take up from where we left off—do as I did a decade ago and put this episode behind us and concentrate on the future."

"I'd like that, too. Very much."

Cayden noticed her eyes were shining. The gleam was back. He placed his arms on the table, palms up. She rested her hands in his.

"I've missed you."

"I've missed you, too."

A single tear slid down Avery's cheek. He wiped it away, his finger lingering on the soft skin he loved to touch. A warm breeze of desire swept over them both.

"What do you say we put these in to-go cups, finish them at my place?"

"I'd say that's a perfect idea."

As Cayden walked to his car, he envisioned ripping off Avery's clothes as soon as the door shut and taking her right there on the floor. It played out differently. Once he held her in his arms, he wanted to savor the reunion. They showered together before making love leisurely, unhurried, rediscovering each other's bodies, appreciating being together again. They talked for hours about everything—Cayden's work, invention and recent dinner in his honor. Avery shared how she'd been freelancing, had secured two clients and was both determined and encouraged to one day follow the dream of starting her own business.

"What would you call it?" he'd asked her. She didn't know. They brainstormed until Cayden suggested, "Events On Point."

Avery loved it. "Sold!"

Over the next month, the two settled into a comfortable flow. While the whirlwind of excitement during their first few weeks of dating had been nice, Cayden appreciated that they'd slowed down and were now taking the time to get to know each other on a deeper level. One Saturday, Cayden treated Avery, Lisa and Tami to dinner and a night of laughter at a new comedy club. Avery joined him for the infamous Eddington brunch, and lived to talk about it. Fall gave way to winter. The holidays arrived. Cayden flew all of them—Avery, Lisa and Lisa's family—to Las Vegas for Thanksgiving. That weekend, back at Cayden's house where Avery basically lived, they enjoyed a relaxing Sunday evening before Cayden was due back at work.

"You know what?" Avery lounged on the couch, half

watching a movie, her feet in Cayden's lap while he surfed on his phone.

"Hmm?"

"You're pretty amazing."

He looked up. "You think so?"

"I know so." Avery shifted to cuddle next to him. "This weekend was everything I could have wanted and just what Lisa and her family needed. I've never seen Frank so animated and Lisa bounced back to the sister I knew before the cancer."

She kissed his cheek. "Thank you."

"You're welcome." He kissed her lips. "Maybe we can invite everyone here for Christmas. Get a huge tree decorated. Lots of presents for Amanda. It would be fun."

Avery sat up. "Hey! I just received a fairly amazing revelation."

Cayden lifted a brow.

"In all our time together, you've never been to my house."

"Is that an invitation?"

"Is that what you were waiting for?"

"You should turn your condo into a rental property. You already practically live here."

"Are you sure we're ready for that?"

"Most definitely." Cayden was starting to believe he was ready for that and much more, but he wasn't ready to tell her that quite yet. "I do want to see your place, though. How one lives says a lot about the person."

"Oh, yeah?" Avery positioned herself on Cayden's lap, and kissed him. "What about how one loves?"

Cayden lifted his hips in a circular motion, grazing

her heat with his dick. "I think I need to do a bit more research before answering that question."

"Will you need any assistance?"

He grabbed her buttocks. "I'll need all of this assistance."

They laughed as he lifted her into his arms and walked to the bedroom where they could more thoroughly help each other—all night long.

Twenty-Four

Cayden followed the GPS instructions and pulled into a visitor parking space at Avery's condo complex. Considering the level of intimacy they'd experienced it felt strange he hadn't been there before. In so many ways his life felt foreign, like it belonged to somebody else. Who was this man working as an executive at a leading financial services company, who'd invented software that would change that whole game, who had an eight-figure payment wired to his bank account a week ago and was a member of one of the most exclusive organizations in the world?

Cayden glanced in the rearview mirror at his reflection. "It's you, dude."

He reached for the ridiculously large bouquet of flowers on the seat beside him, then exited the car and followed the sidewalk to Avery's address and rang the doorbell. He felt the beat of his heart increase. In many ways, this felt like a first date. The door opened. He played it cool on the outside, but inside, his heart skipped a beat. He got a premonition that he was looking into his future.

"Hello." He emphasized the second syllable, his eyes conducting an appreciative head-to-toe.

"Hey, Cayden."

"You look beautiful."

"Thank you."

He glimpsed an unreadable emotion in her eyes before they shifted to the flowers. "Wow! That bouquet is stunning and...huge!"

"It's my first time visiting your home. Plus, it's the holiday season. Seemed to fit the moment."

"I've got the perfect vase," she said with a shyness in her voice that was as sexy as hell. "Come on in."

He stepped inside and managed a quick kiss and half hug around the bouquet.

A few steps into her living room, she whirled around. "I've got to admit something. I'm nervous. I know it's crazy but—"

"No, it's not." Cayden let out a relieved chuckle. She smiled. "Walking up to your door felt like a first date."

"We are doing the very common dinner and a movie."

"Which we've never done before."

"I know, right? On local dates we've mostly hung out at your house."

"Same with choosing the flowers. Seemed fitting."

"Let's put them over here. I'll get a vase."

Cayden watched the moon rise in the form of her swaying ass as she placed the flowers on the dining room table and then continued down the hall. Once he was able to pull his eyes away, he took in what he could see from the partially open layout. The home felt very much like Avery—classy, soothing, understated. He liked that her home wasn't pretentious and appreciated the neutral palette with just enough splash of color to make the rooms interesting.

She returned holding a sizable vase. "This will be perfect." She removed a uniquely tied silk ribbon from the bouquet before placing it into the urn-like porcelain.

"You're right. It's just the right size."

"It's my first time using it." After arranging the flowers, Avery stepped back. A warm, sweet smile spread across her face.

"What are you thinking?"

"It's the first time I've used the vase to actually hold flowers. A regular bouquet gets swallowed up."

Cayden took a step closer. His hands itched to be around her waist. His lips craved the feel of hers.

"It's beautiful."

Avery turned to him. "It belonged to my mother." Her eyes dropped to his lips, then back to his eyes as her head leaned toward his. "Thank you."

The kiss was feathery light, but with enough electricity to power metro LA. Cayden pulled Avery into his embrace, his tongue silently demanding to deepen the exchange. He felt her nipples pebble against him and caressed each one with his thumbs. Avery groaned into his mouth, her hands rubbing his back and down his ass. He pressed his rapidly hardening shaft against her leg. She abruptly ended the kiss, taking a breath as she stepped back.

"I have a feeling that…if we don't stop now…"

"We might not make that dinner and a movie?"

"Exactly."

"I'm fine with takeout and Movie Reel on the Net." Cayden reached for her hand. "But you've gotten all dressed up and look so amazing, it would be a shame not to share a bit of this hot vision with Chicago on such a cold night."

"All right now, my multicultural brother. You'd better bottle it up and sell that swag!"

"I'm serious!"

Laughing, she gave him another quick hug. "Let me grab my purse."

Once in Cayden's car and on the way, Avery asked, "Where are you taking me?"

"That new place over on Near South Side."

"No way! We're going to Sol to Sol?" Cayden nodded, happy to see her reaction. "I was just online with them last week. Reservations are six months out."

"Unless you know somebody who knows somebody…"

"Is it that SOMA power? I'm impressed."

The New Age–themed restaurant with a prix fixe menu had the perfect atmosphere for love. There were only twelve tables, separated by half-walls and luscious plants to afford guests at least partial privacy. The host seated them by a window that offered a view of the holiday lights from buildings across downtown, with Lake Michigan an inky expanse beyond it. Not long after, a sommelier appeared with the night's sparkling wine, a top-shelf, vintage brut, selected to complement the meat and fish entrées.

Cayden held up his glass.

Avery followed suit. "What are we toasting to this time?"

"I performed the toast on the plane, remember? Tonight, it's your turn." Cayden knew the raspiness in his voice signaled how much he desired Avery right now and he did not give one damn. By the way she squirmed, it appeared she received the message.

"Let's toast to…this. Tonight. Us. Whatever it means and whatever it brings. And," she hurried on before he could take a sip. "Once again to your amazing year. Launching AI Interface. Becoming a member of SOMA. Achieving just one of those goals would have been ginormous. These achievements are bigger than that and couldn't happen to a more deserving individual. A man of integrity and grace. I love you."

"Wow, babe. Thank you." Cayden leaned over for a kiss. Avery happily obliged.

The appetizers arrived—roasted Brussels sprouts and Vidalia onions in a maple bacon glaze. For the next ninety minutes, Cayden and Avery were treated to the remarkable culinary skills of a young, creative, talented chef. During and in between courses, they touched on subjects and people meaningful to both of them. The Point Country Club and their "special" town. Lisa's "all-clear" checkup. Tami, Cayden's adopted family, the Eddingtons, and Avery's next freelance client, an engagement party next month.

"I thought you weren't going to book anymore until after the new year."

"This was a referral. It fell in my lap. The party is relatively small, her wishes are manageable and her budget is major. A perfect way to get my name out there and add to my résumé. I couldn't pass it up."

"Experience for when you have your own agency?"

"It'll probably be years before that can happen, but yeah, maybe someday."

After ending the evening with a flourish—a hot fudge sundae for two topped with fresh fruit, Venezuelan Chuao chocolate, sweet Grand Passion caviar and gold-coated almonds—the couple joined hands as they headed outside. Night had fallen and the temperatures along with it. Cayden wrapped his arms around Avery and pulled her back against him.

"I need to ask the chef where he got that chocolate syrup."

"It was delicious."

"Yeah, but not half as tasty as it would be if I were licking it off you."

The valet arrived with their car. They hurried to get inside its warmth. Cayden took off, slowly cruising as they took in the surrounding holiday decorations. He reached an intersection with an on-ramp to the freeway. Instead of taking it, however, he continued straight before turning at the next light.

"Where are we going now?"

"I want to show you something."

"Is it something that I can see from the car? It feels like below zero out there."

"Yeah." He glanced over, his grin slight and cocky. "You're going to have to get out."

"You might have to snap a picture. Let me see it on your phone."

They reached the parking lot of a tall corner building that was once a hotel. The bottom floors had been converted into commercial properties. Lights flickered from decorated windows and trees. The night was quiet. Cayden pulled into the parking lot and a reserved space.

"We're going in here?"

"Yes."

"Are you sure, Cayden? It didn't look like any of those places were open."

"I've got the hookup."

"Hookup for what?" she asked as he opened her door.

"For whatever I want you to see. Come on, woman!"

"It's frickin' freezing!"

"Don't worry. I'll warm that fine ass up in a minute. Now, come on."

Cayden pulled out a key as they neared the back entrance.

"I was right. Everything's closed."

"Which is why I told you that I had the hookup."

Avery tried to huff softly, but he heard her.

"Are you mad?"

"I'm cold."

The annoyance amused him. He opened the door. A blast of warm air greeted them.

"Better?"

She nodded. "Much."

He placed a hand at her elbow. "It's this way."

They walked down a hall with brick walls, exposed pipes and dark hardwood floors. Avery ran her hand across an office door with beveled glass. "How'd you find this place?"

"Buddy of mine manages the building. We came through the employee entrance for these flexible work spaces and the shops up front."

"I love the unfinished aesthetic. Clearly it's been renovated and updated but the original character of the building is still here."

"I thought you'd like it." They turned down another hall and through a door that led to the front shops. He unlocked the door to the first business, a corner property, then guided Avery into the darkened room.

"Wait here while I find the light switch. Don't move. Things may have been rearranged since the last time I was here."

"Okay."

Cayden took a few steps along the wall and felt for the plate near the corner. After finding it he flicked on the light, turned to her and said, "Open your eyes."

The feeling was indescribable as he watched Avery's eyes take in the contemporary furniture in the reception area before traveling up to a sign on the wall:

Events On Point
by Avery Gray

Her eyes widened as she stared at the sign. For several seconds she didn't move. Cayden wondered if she was breathing. She slowly turned to look at him, her face a ball of confusion.

"How did…? What…?" She looked at the sign. "That's my company's name!"

Cayden walked to stand beside her. He placed an arm around her waist and observed the sign, too.

"Hmm. That is the name I came up with, huh?"

"Yes! Another Chicago company already has it? Damn. I loved that name, remember?"

"Come to think of it, I do remember." He managed not to smile but his eyes were gleaming.

Avery left where they were standing and walked farther into the space. It contained a large central area, a break/meeting room and two small offices. Pendant lighting hung from the tall ceiling where recessed fixtures had been installed, as well. The large front and side bay windows were great for dressing and would let in tons of natural daylight.

She came back to where Cayden stood watching her, a smile threatening to erupt from both sides of his mouth.

Avery's eyes narrowed. "What's going on?"

"What do you mean?"

"Uh-uh. Don't give me that innocent look. You've got to know something. You brought me here! Aside from that furniture—" she nodded toward the reception area "—and the conference table, the place is empty. And on top of that, my name, along with the one you thought up for the company that's not even been created yet, is on the wall."

She crossed her arm. "Okay. I get it. You've got jokes."

"Me?"

"Your friend manages the building. You obviously had the sign printed and got him to put it up. Thanks, babe. I didn't need the motivation but seeing that sign is pretty cool. Kinda makes it real. Like it really is possible."

She continued, examining the room once again, "I mean, this space would be perfect. The offices. That meeting room would be great for presentations. This space—" she spread her arms to take in the area "—would be a small yet quiet and efficient showroom. Is this place available for rent? Is that why you brought me here?"

"Wow, you love it that much?"

"Like I said, it's perfect. Not that it matters. I'm a long way from being able to open my own business."

She walked over, put her arms around his neck and kissed him. "But thanks, though. Thanks for believing in my dream and setting this up. That was very thoughtful. In fact—" she stepped back and pulled out her phone

"—I'm going to take a picture of that sign, have it framed and put it on the wall in my home office. That single picture will be my vision board."

He watched her take several pictures of the sign and the space. Unable to keep up the ruse any longer, he reached into his other pocket before sidling up behind her. "I've got a better idea," he murmured in her ear.

She turned in his arms, holding him close once again. "What's that?"

"This." He held up a heart-shaped key chain that held several keys. Avery stared at the keys, dumbfounded and speechless.

"The keys to your business," he explained.

Avery took a stunned step away from him. Her mouth opened but no words came out.

"That's if you're sure this space will work."

Finally, Avery's mind and mouth got on the same wavelength. She spoke while circling the room, ending back up in front of him. "I think this space would be amazing, Cayden, but even with your friend managing the building, and even with a discount, I couldn't afford the rent here. This is one of the most desired areas for up-and-coming businesses in the entire metropolitan area! I'm surprised the space is empty. I could never afford it."

"Don't worry." Cayden pulled her into his arms and kissed her forehead. "I'm sure you can work something out with the owner."

Her eyes narrowed. "You didn't buy this building."

"I thought it would be a great investment. The entire structure has tons of potential. But this space is my gift to you, rent-free. Merry Christmas."

"Merry…" Tears began to shimmer in Avery's eyes as she stared at him, the reality of what he'd done sink-ing in. "You're saying I can use this space to set up my business?"

"Yes. Set it up and run it…for as long as you want."

"Oh, my gosh! Are you serious? I can't believe this. Thank you," she said, placing her arms around his neck and kisses all over his face. "It's the most amazing gift anyone has ever given me."

She released him to check out the other spaces. He followed her, listening as she began decorating the rooms in her mind. They reached the smaller of the two offices, tucked away from the large front windows. Cayden pulled Avery to him and began easing off her coat.

"You know what we've got to do, right?"

"What?"

He turned her so that he could unzip her dress. "The space isn't really yours until it's been christened."

"What are you doing?" Avery asked, even as she slid out of her heels.

"I'm undressing you. And I think you know why."

"You're such a naughty boy."

"Baby girl, you ain't seen nothin' yet." He removed his slacks. The evidence of his desire strained the front of his boxers.

"I love you, Avery Gray."

She ran her hand along his length, reached inside and brushed her fingers across the sensitive skin. He hissed. She smiled.

"I love you, too."

The lovemaking was uninhibited and inventive. Much later, when getting dressed, they laughed and joked with the carefreeness of those kids back in high school when Cayden was the basketballer, shot caller, and Avery held a secret crush.

"I'll never forget this," she said as they stepped out of the warm hallway into the chilly winter Chicago night.

Cayden thought about the set of rings being designed by Audra Lee Covington, the famous jeweler to the stars, and smiled as he opened her door.

"I'm sure there will be other memorable moments," he said, starting the car and rubbing cold hands together.

Like in the not-too-distant future when I ask you to become my wife.

He'd planned a Valentine getaway to their favorite Southern California winery, where he'd pop the question. Everything about the year had been amazing. Next year would be even better. Dream job. Dream new product. Dream woman. Dream life. For sure, Cayden's life was on point.

* * * * *

#2845 MARRIED BY CONTRACT
Texas Cattleman's Club: Fathers and Sons
by Yvonne Lindsay
Burned before, rancher Gabriel Carrington wants a marriage on paper. But when one hot night with fashionista Rosalind Banks ends in pregnancy, he proposes...a deal. Their marriage of convenience could give them both what they want—if they can get past their sizzling chemistry...

#2846 ONE LITTLE SECRET
Dynasties: The Carey Center • by Maureen Child
Branching out from his wealthy family, black sheep Justin Carey pursued a business deal with hotelier Sadie Harris, when things turned hot fast. Meeting a year later, he's shocked by the secret she's kept. Can things remain professional when the attraction's still there?

#2847 THE PERFECT FAKE DATE
Billionaires of Boston • by Naima Simone
Learning he's the secret heir to a business mogul, Kenan Rhodes has a lot to prove. He asks best friend and lingerie designer Eve Burke to work with him, and she agrees...if he'll help her sharpen her dating skills. Soon, fake dates lead to sexy nights...

#2848 RETURN OF THE RANCHER
by Janice Maynard
After their passionate whirlwind marriage ended five years ago, India Lamont is shocked when her mysterious ex, businessman Farris Quinn, invites her to his Wyoming ranch to help his ailing mother. The attraction's still there...and so are his long-held secrets...

#2849 THE BAD BOY EXPERIMENT
The Bourbon Brothers • by Reese Ryan
When real estate developer Cole Abbott's high school crush returns to town, she has him rethinking his no-commitment stance. So when newly divorced Renee Lockwood proposes a no-strings fling, he's in. As things turn serious, will this fiery love affair turn into forever?

#2850 TALL, DARK AND OFF LIMITS
Men of Maddox Hill • by Shannon McKenna
Responsible for Maddox Hill Architecture's security, Zack Austin takes his job very seriously. Unfortunately, his best friend and the CEO's sister, Ava Maddox, has a talent for finding trouble. When Ava needs his help, he must ignore every bit of their undeniable attraction...

SPECIAL EXCERPT FROM

ⒽHARLEQUIN

DESIRE

*Learning he's the secret heir to a business mogul,
Kenan Rhodes has a lot to prove. His best friend,
lingerie designer Eve Burke, agrees to work with him...
if he'll help her sharpen her dating skills.
Soon, fake dates lead to sexy nights...*

Read on for a sneak peek of
The Perfect Fake Date,
by USA TODAY *bestselling author Naima Simone.*

The corridor ended, and he stood in front of another set of
towering doors. Kenan briefly hesitated, then grasped the
handle, opened the doors and slipped through to the balcony
beyond. The cool April night air washed over him. The
calendar proclaimed spring had arrived, but winter hadn't
yet released its grasp over Boston, especially at night. But he
welcomed the chilled breeze over his face, let it seep beneath
the confines of his tuxedo to the hot skin below. Hoped it
could cool the embers of his temper...the still-burning coals
of his hurt.

"For someone who is known as the playboy of Boston
society, you sure will ditch a party in a hot second." Slim arms
slid around him, and he closed his eyes in pain and pleasure as
the petite, softly curved body pressed to his back. "All I had
to do was follow the trail of longing glances from the women
in the hall to figure out where you'd gone."

He snorted. "Do you lie to your mama with that mouth?
There was hardly anyone out there."

"Fine," Eve huffed. "So I didn't go with the others and
watched all of that go down with your parents and brother. I
waited until you left the ballroom and went after you."

"Why?" he rasped.

He felt rather than witnessed her shrug. The same with the small kiss she pressed to the middle of his shoulder blades. He locked his muscles, forcing his head not to fall back. Ordering his throat to imprison the moan scrabbling up from his chest. Commanding his dick to stand down.

"Because you needed me," she said.

So simple. So goddamn true.

He did need her. Her friendship. Her body.

Her heart.

But since he could only have one of those, he'd take it. With a woman like her—generous, sweet, beautiful of body and spirit—even part of her was preferable to none of her. And if he dared to profess his true feelings, that was exactly what he would be left with. None of her. Their friendship would be ruined, and she was too important to him to risk losing her.

Carefully, he turned and wrapped her in his embrace, shielding her from the night air. Convincing himself if this was all he could have of her—even if it meant Gavin would have all of her—then he would be okay, he murmured, "You're really going to have to remove 'rescue best friend' off your résumé. For one, it's beginning to get too time-consuming. And two, the cape clashes with your gown."

She chuckled against his chest, tipping her head back to smile up at him. He curled his fingers against her spine, but that didn't prevent the ache to trace that sensual bottom curve.

"Where would be the fun in that? You're stuck with me, Kenan. And I'm stuck with you. Friends forever."

Friends.

The sweet sting of that knife buried between his ribs.

"Always, sweetheart."

Don't miss what happens next in
The Perfect Fake Date *by Naima Simone,*
the next book in the Billionaires of Boston series!

Available January 2022 wherever
Harlequin Desire books and ebooks are sold.

Harlequin.com

HDEXP1221

Get 4 FREE REWARDS!

We'll send you 2 FREE Books plus <u>2 FREE Mystery Gifts.</u>

Harlequin Desire books transport you to the world of the American elite with juicy plot twists, delicious sensuality and intriguing scandal.

FREE Value Over $20

Sierra Crane cringed every time her ex-husband called.
Their marriage had ended almost two years ago, so why
couldn't he get on with his life the way she had gotten on
with hers? This was the second phone call in a month.

"What is it now, Nathan?" she asked.

"You know what I want, Sierra. We rushed into our
divorce and I want a reconciliation. We didn't even seek
counseling."

She rolled her eyes. She had put up with things for as
long as she could. His infidelity had been the last straw.

"Why are we even discussing this? You know as well
as I do that no amount of counseling would have helped
our marriage. You betrayed me. I caught you in the act.
Look, I'm busy. Goodbye."

Sierra glanced at the door and saw Vaughn Miller walk
in, dressed in a business suit.

She didn't know Vaughn personally, although they
had both been born in Catalina Cove and attended the
same schools. She hadn't had the right pedigree to be
in his social circles since his family had been one of the
wealthiest in town.

When Vaughn took a seat, she grabbed a menu and
headed to his table.

"Welcome to the Green Fig."

He looked up when she handed him the menu. "Thanks."

This was the closest she had ever been to Vaughn Miller, and she couldn't help noticing things she hadn't seen from a distance. Like the beautiful hazel coloring of his eyes. He had sharp cheekbones and full lips. And she couldn't miss the light beard that covered his lower jaw but didn't hide the dimple in his chin.

Vaughn's skin was a maple brown and he wore his thick black hair long enough to touch his collar.

She knew six years ago he'd been sent to prison for a crime he didn't commit. Three months ago newspaper articles reported on his exoneration. He had been cleared of all charges.

"What's the special for today?"

She blinked upon realizing she'd been staring at him. Clearing her throat, she told him.

His smile made his features even more beguiling. "That sounds good. I'd like a bowl with a chicken sandwich."

Sierra nodded. "Okay, I'll put in your order."

"Thanks."

She turned and walked toward the kitchen. When she knew she was out of his sight and that of the customers and staff, she fanned herself with the menu. Vaughn Miller had definitely made every hormone in her body sizzle.

Don't miss what happens next in…
One Christmas Wish
by Brenda Jackson.
Available October 2021 wherever
HQN books and ebooks are sold.

HQNBooks.com